Fourteen Hills
THE SAN FRANCISCO STATE UNIVERSITY REVIEW

THE SAN FRANCISCO STATE UNIVERSITY REVIEW

No. 28

2022

Fourteen Hills Press
San Francisco

A very special thanks to the following individuals, whose efforts made this issue of *Fourteen Hills* possible: Jane George; Nona Caspers; Chet Wiener; and Nicole Baxter, Devin Koch, and the team at Bookmobile.

Cover artwork: "Dolabela Engineer" by Guilherme Bergamini.
Typesetting, book design, and cover design by James Giffin.

ISBN: 978-1-889292-83-0

© 2022 Department of Creative Writing, College of Liberal and Creative Arts, San Francisco State University. All rights revert to contributors. No part of this journal may be reproduced or transmitted in any form or by any means, electronic or mechanical, including photocopying, recording, or by any information storage and retrieval system, without written permission from the authors, except for the inclusion of brief quotations in a review.

Printed by Bookmobile, Inc. in the USA.

Published annually by Fourteen Hills Press.
San Francisco State University / Dept. of Creative Writing
1600 Holloway Ave. / San Francisco, CA 94132
www.14hills.net

Distributed by Small Press Distribution.
1341 Seventh St. / Berkeley, CA 94710
www.spdbooks.org

Individual subscriptions: one year for $16 or two years for $32. Back issues are $5 each.

Submissions: the submission period runs from February 15th to June 15th. All submissions are electronic. Details at www.14hills.net.

Erratum: in our previous issue, we misspelled the title of Turandot Shayegan's poem "Taxes & God." At *Fourteen Hills*, we understand that such differences, however small, can change the reader's perception of a work and sincerely apologize for our error.

THE SAN FRANCISCO STATE UNIVERSITY REVIEW

No. 28
2022

EDITORS-IN-CHIEF
Quinn Rennerfeldt Fairchild
Estrellita "Sen" Ruíz

MANAGING EDITOR
Jack Darrow

POETRY EDITOR
Lillian Giles

FICTION EDITORS
Victor Baeza
Hellen Keshishian

ASSISTANT POETRY EDITORS
Michaela Chairez
Elizabeth Hoover
Gizzel Adriana Yanez

ASSISTANT FICTION EDITORS
Chris Jones
Tadeh Kennedy

NONFICTION EDITOR
Cyril Sebastian

DESIGN & NONFICTION EDITOR
James Giffin

P.R. & MARKETING EDITORS
Kato Bisase
Chandler Fitchett

ART EDITOR
Kristen Wong

FACULTY ADVISORS
Carolina De Robertis
Michael David Lukas

EDITORIAL STAFF
Angelina Bidema   August Edwards
Michael Gallagher   Larae Mays-Hardy
Jasmine Mosher   Jarrett Turner
Peter Xiong

CONTENTS

nonfiction

BLIND SPOTS, *Amber Wong*	1
PERFORMANCE NOTES, *Patrick Kindig*	107

fiction

LEAVING BOYSTOWN, *Mary Lynn Reed*	15
THE DEVIL'S CHORD, *Candice Wuehle*	29
RAGER, *Ronald Koertge*	37
CRIMES AGAINST THE PEACE OF THE STATE, *Sean Maschmann*	47
TRANSFUSION, *A. A. deFreese*	57
SIENA DIARIES, *Angie Cruz*, 2021 Gina Berriault Award recipient	61
ETTO, 1959, *Cameron Moreno*	77
EDDIE'S MOM, *Ciaran Cooper*	85
GANAP, *Liz Iversen*	99
MRS. D'SOUZA'S MANGO TREE, *Hema Padhu*	113
ARCHAEOLOGY, *Jacques Denault*	124
ALOE, *Andrew Porter*	137

poetry

GENESIS, *Erin Wilson*	12
HAND OF GOD, *Stefan Karlsson*	25
BROKEN SONNET FOR THE AMERICAN SCHOOLGIRL, *Mary Henn*	34
ODE TO A MAKESHIFT HEROIN PIPE, *Mary Henn*	35
HOME VIDEOS TELLS US AGAIN, *Mary Henn*	36
THE OBJECT WORLD IS SMALL, *Sean Cho A.*	43
THE END OF THE NOVEL, *Laura Ritland*	45
PREPAREDNESS, *Alex Wells Shapiro*	56
APHORISM 30, *John Blair*	59
RESURRECTION, *Natasha Huey*	70
WHO IS AN INDIVIDUAL, *Natasha Huey*	72
A NAME, *Natasha Huey*	73
HIRAETH, *Catherine Kyle*	79
GLITTER CAMO GIRL, *Catherine Kyle*	80
LE MACHINNE, *Megan Erickson*	96
THE BOY WHO LIVES IN DREAMS, *Saúl Hernández*	105
MAGIC IN THE HISS, *Ashleigh A. Allen*	111
PALINODE, *B.P. Sutton*, 2022 Stacy Doris Memorial Poetry Award recipient	127
__HUATL, *Art Por Díaz*	139

visual art

CATFISH, *Nathan Kosta*	27
SYSTEMATIC THEOLOGY, *Don Swartzentruber*	28
KNOW YOURSELF, *Valeria Amirkhanyan*	75
MOTH MOUNTAIN, *Kate Gardiner*	76
THE DOORS OF PERCEPTION IN PALESTINE, *Nicholas Karavatos*	97
DOLABELA ENGINEER, *Guilherme Bergamini*	125
FUSCA RED, *Guilherme Bergamini*	126
CHECK POINT WALL #1, *Nicholas Karavatos*	126

special feature:
neurodivergent, black-and-white visual art

STAIRS, *Christopher Strople*	64
TRESTLES, *Christopher Strople*	65
POND, *Christopher Strople*	65
DARKNESS LOOMS #3, *Edward Michael Supranowicz*	66
DARKNESS LOOMS #4, *Edward Michael Supranowicz*	66
WHAT LIES BENEATH, *Grace Wagner*	67
ROCOCO DREAMS, *Grace Wagner*	68
DAMN SPOT, *Grace Wagner*	69

CONTRIBUTORS   143

Fourteen Hills

BLIND SPOTS
Amber Wong

When I offered myself up as the token minority, I rolled my eyes and thought, "*Somebody's* got to do it." In August 2020, the idea of having an all-white diversity committee at our Seattle rowing club bordered on satire: too earnest, too oxymoronic to be taken seriously. To be honest, I'd laughed when I first heard about it. Then I felt sheepish. Then I volunteered.

Sitting in my home office, in the lull before the other three committee members joined our weekly Zoom call, I chatted with the young guy leading the committee. We're a generation apart but found something in common: he currently works for the federal government. Before my retirement ten years ago, I did too.

Knowing that his agency, with oversight over mine, was traditionally a wary adversary, I broached what I hoped was a benign topic. "So is your agency unionized?" I asked. That had been a huge human resources headache facing the Environmental Protection Agency management team as I was leaving government. Some job classifications were being unionized while others were not. As managers, we wondered how we could treat everyone equitably if the union imposed certain conditions on dealing with "their" people.

"Yes," he said matter-of-factly, as if it had always been that way. "Why?"

I started to explain that unionizing the professional staff had once been controversial. "Well, when I was a manager at the EPA, we were trying to figure out how that would work. You see—"

He broke in, "Oh? You were a manager?"

Thwap. I felt my eyes narrow while the rest of my body flinched. Why was he surprised? Had he just reframed me as the enemy, a symbol of the historic distrust between unions and management? Or maybe he was thinking, "Ah, this explains her bossy attitude." Or worse: he may be revealing a deep implicit bias—he didn't envision Asian Americans, especially women, in management. Was it our well-documented lack of representation—he'd never seen a female Asian American manager before? Had he bought into the model minority stereotype of Asian Americans as hard workers with excellent technical skills, but not powerful enough to lead? Damn the media. Too few Asians have been portrayed with the strengths that characterize leaders in white America. No wonder "management material" doesn't leap to mind.

But his comment cut deeper than it should. It felt more personal. Today's social landscape may have primed me to take offense, to instinctively condemn him for being insensitive. But was I being unfair, too judgmental? He knew nothing of my history, my family's generations of banging on citizenship's iron gates, being told, "We'd hire you/promote you/let you live in our neighborhood/let you join our club if you weren't Chinese." He couldn't appreciate how long it took me, a Chinese American girl coming of age in the 1960s, to overcome my culture's throttling expectation to be seen but not heard. He couldn't know how hard it was for me to even aspire to be a manager, to breach those cultural barriers, when my every success was weighted by my parents' demands to do better, work harder, be the best, because I had to be at least twice as good as a white person to get ahead. He'd never feel the schism of identity—the secret guilty pride of believing I could be the first in my family to crack the bamboo ceiling—if only I could cast aside its accompanying accusation: "You're becoming too white!"

But if assimilation has taught me one thing, it's to pump the brakes on my outrage. If I turn offensive, I'll never get my message across, because other people's ears can slam as shut as mine have. So I paused to reframe the situation, offer the benefit of the doubt: *Did he sound incredulous, or was that just in my head?*

When I was a manager in the late 1990s, the federal government issued a report about the dearth of Asian American managers in federal service[1]. At least that's how I interpreted it. The report listed pay grades for Asian Americans across all federal agencies, and as expected, Asian Americans were clumped at the staff and administrative levels. The same was true in our 680-person office. Three of us were managers, and despite glowing performance reviews and multiple attempts, none would ever make it to the executive team.

Years later, when I heard of a program aimed at correcting this inequality, I knew I had to visit[2].

In 2015, from the back of a well-lit classroom at the Stanford Graduate School of Business, I looked across a sea of black hair. Never had I seen a classroom like this. So many Asians! I hummed with excitement. Seated before me were forty senior managers from a wide swath of companies: tech start-ups, international banks, and large firms with immediately recognizable logos. Ranging in age from early thirties to mid-fifties, these women and men had been tapped by their companies as people with potential, poised to hit the board room, aimed for the executive ranks. Here to attend Stanford University's week-long Asian American Executive Program, they were ready to crush the bamboo ceiling to the C-suite. In their casual Friday workwear, they looked comfortable yet confident. I longed to be one of them, but for me it was too late. I was here to observe, to listen, and to hope.

Program founders Buck Gee and Wes Hom were both born in the United States—one in California, one in New York—to Chinese immigrant families. Both grew up dirt poor. But higher education at Stanford, Harvard, and NYU, plus ambition, catapulted them from working class to the C-suite. Late in their careers, just before retiring from Cisco and IBM as vice presidents, they looked around the executive ranks of their companies and those they dealt with and saw themselves alone. "Where are the rest of us?" they asked. Like them, many Asian Americans had joined tech companies after college, but unlike them, never seemed to get beyond the ranks of middle management. Why were they all stalling out? Post-retirement, Gee and Hom surveyed five prominent Silicon Valley tech firms where nearly half of the workforce was Asian American. Their informal observations were confirmed: Asian American men comprised only 13.5% of the executives, while Asian American women comprised a mere 3.1%[3]. The Asian American "bamboo ceiling" was almost four times worse than the much-hyped "glass ceiling" for women. So they decided to do something about it. Working with Hayagreeva "Huggy" Rao, a Stanford professor as warm as his name, they developed the Asian American Executive Program[4].

The program, established in 2010, aims to train Asian Americans in the social skills needed to thrive in corporate America. Some of the common gaps they found: expectations of leaders and leadership, ability to speak up in meetings, openly debating with one's manager, and taking big risks. While these behaviors are culturally difficult for many Asian Americans, companies also bear some responsibility to notice and develop minority employees into leaders and executives.

I can't tell you the specifics of the program, but I can tell you this: if it had existed twenty years ago, I'd have clamored to attend. If I'd been tapped, I'd be ecstatic. It would have been a potent symbol, a clear declaration, an affirmation: We see you.

∽

Joining the boathouse's diversity committee felt transgressive, like whining out loud. As a fourth-generation Chinese American with hardscrabble ancestors in the California mining, laundry, gambling, and finally, professional ranks, I was raised to ignore racial slights, to rise above it all. Calling out prejudice and admitting how carefully we had to navigate white America was scorned as "playing the race card." As weak. Yet recently I've grasped that denying my ethnicity doesn't erase it, nor does it allow me to be fully seen as a friend, as a worker, even as a rower. So my internal debate about joining the committee ended, as usual, on a rational argument: representation. Perhaps I could amplify the credibility of the committee by adding my voice and lived experience to the mix.

Yet even within this safe space I strain to make myself heard.

Partly it's the nature of this sport. Crew is singularly white. Tagged from inception as an elitist, Ivy League, ultra-competitive pursuit, rowing is only now recognizing a need to undo its history of exclusion. I picture my third-generation American dad, an athletic, six-foot-tall, Boston University medical student in the 1950s, watching the world-renowned, highly competitive Head of the Charles Regatta from a bridge spanning the Charles River. Marveling at the historic pageantry of the race, cheering for every BU team streaming by, he would never have deigned to think he could break into that old white boys' club.

Then there's demographics. Fifty years later, when I first stepped into a Seattle boathouse with my biracial teenage son for his introductory learn-to-row class, I felt the sniff of its country club aura. The donor wall plaque was etched with names that were not like mine. Pictures on the walls honored people who didn't look like me. Yet I expected nothing different. My circle of friends, my workplaces, my neighborhood communities are, and always have been, virtually all white. Federal laws from 1882 to 1965[5,6] effectively restricted Asian immigration, so throughout my childhood, there were very few Chinese Americans. The 1960 US Census counted only 237,000 of us in a total population of 179,300,000. A miniscule 0.13%. Therefore, to steel myself against being treated like a perpetual curiosity, to will myself into ignoring any stares or whispered asides, I pretend to blend in until someone points out that I don't. This uneasy truce requires an exquisite balance of poise and suspicion, a snap judgment: *Am I safe here?* After a quick read of the raftered, sweat-steeped boathouse amidst a throng of chatty parents and their teens, I was more conscious of being a single mom than anything else. I catalogued the lack of diversity as a given. I noticed it like I noticed that most rowers were over six feet tall. What I noticed was my 6'1" son who passes for white would fit in.

Turns out, Bryce shone at crew for two years, rising directly from novice to varsity. He became disciplined about time management. His grades improved. In 2008, he and his team qualified for and rowed a 4+ at the Head of the Charles Regatta, about which I was proud beyond reason. Jumping up and down among a deafening crowd on a bridge spanning the Charles River, I watched his boat surge toward me with tears streaming down my face. Sweeping away my father's existential angst felt like a burden lifted, a promise kept. Our family's century-and-a-half commitment to America was paying off. In the thrill of that moment, I was convinced America loved us back.

I was so overcome with gratitude that weeks later, when Bryce abruptly announced he was done with rowing—choosing late night music gigs over 6 a.m. rows—I didn't argue. I told myself that he'd reached a pinnacle, a personal best. And, I noted guiltily, a family best. His rowing the Head of the Charles checked so many boxes. In the whitest of white spaces, we'd finally breached those iron gates. Take *that*, America! We belong.

Yet there was more. As "Bryce's mom," I'd become embedded, even welcomed, into the rowing community. And that's when I became a rower.

Bryce turns thirty this year. After college he lived in the downtown hubs of Portland, New York, and Philadelphia, where inclusion was a given and "oppression tokens"—markers of marginalization—were applauded and valued. Now that he's temporarily landed in rural Virginia, he's living in an alternate universe, a jolting reminder of the chasm between social factions in America. But his lived experience is valuable. I can talk to him more honestly about race and identity than I can with anyone else.

On a FaceTime call, he slides his headphones off his hipster mop of brown hair and settles them around his neck. He's recording in his music studio, the one he set up in his closet in Virginia. With a guitar perched on his lap, he looks tired but happy. Behind him I see frayed thrift-store clothes on hangers. Not only does the fabric muffle the sound for his neighbors, it also cuts out background noise while he records. Seeing him in the cramped confines of the closet is oddly reassuring. Also reassuring—in the shape of his eyes is a hint of me.

His quizzical smile reminds me of my dad, now long gone. "So, what's this about the boathouse diversity committee?" Our shared understanding of boathouse culture makes this an easy entry. "Everyone knows that crew is white. And elitist."

"Well, we're trying to figure out how to make it less white. And less elitist."

He snorts. "Good luck with that."

"I *know*. I've told them that even if the boathouse becomes more welcoming, minorities may still not want to join. If you've been code-switching all day at work, why subject yourself to another all-white space for recreation? Especially when surrounded by that air of elitism."

"Yeah, you make it sound so appealing." We laugh together. I'm warmed by his humor, happy to speak freely.

"Well, here's what's *not* appealing about being on the committee," I say. I mention the almost singular focus on recruiting and retaining Black rowers. "What about the rest of us?"

As the words leave my mouth, I'm aware I'm conflicted. I know that the Black community has led the historic struggle for civil rights, lifting all minorities, but I also don't want other POC's experiences to be discounted in comparison. This is not a competition on who drew the worst hand, a pointless argument that only pits us against each other. Suddenly the source of my irritation becomes clear; on this committee, it's personal. I want—no, *need*—to see myself in our definition of diversity. In this space, and all others, I don't want to be dismissed as "almost white." Because when white people see Asian Americans as white-adjacent, they can completely disregard our existence, minimize our struggle, nullify our fraught and horrific history in this country. They can whitewash my family's truth of America.

Bryce nods. "Yeah, that's so typical. America's conversation on race is stuck in the Black/white binary," he says, and I could kiss him for validating my point of view.

Eagerly I add, "Even some of my *progressive* friends don't get it. When white people chime in with anecdotes of how they felt when they were the 'minority' in the room, I want to slap them and tell them they're missing the point."

"Yeah, that's a false analogy," Bryce groans. "Turns out that the experience of being a minority within a microcosm of society is not comparable to the experience being a minority within the macro setting. Both inside and outside the room, they know they're still white, with all the power that comes with it."

I do a double take. He said *they*. Who is *he*? Is he a wily chameleon, able to take on my cloak of color when he talks with me, even as he understands the privilege that comes from being white? Or my honest arbiter, helping me to calibrate my feelings between those two worlds? Maybe, as a millennial, he could help me understand the guy on the diversity committee.

I tell Bryce the details of our exchange. When I finish, he shrugs and says, "Well, only you and he can speak to the type of tone he used. Sometimes

I tell someone I grew up in Seattle and their response is, 'Oh, you're from Seattle?' They aren't incredulous, just curious."

I frown. That's not what I want to hear. I press harder.

"But, 'Oh, you were a manager?'" I exaggerate my tone for effect, then drop to my normal register. "Even if I were white, that sounds like he's questioning my competence. Besides, he should be aware that a comment like that to a POC carries some different weight."

"Yeah, that's more problematic," he concedes. "But the idea of someone having to compulsively screen their language just to engage in a conversation with a POC seems depressing."

Why is he siding with *them*? I jut out my lower lip, a pout. "That's why I was taught to never bring it up. Don't want to make other people feel bad."

Silence.

Humor often exposes deeper truth. Bryce senses my distress, and I'm startled at how close to the surface it has come. The fog between us breaks. In the space between thoughts and feelings, our discussion suddenly flips from a purely intellectual exercise to a lived-in-the-skin reality. He sees me slipping. Seams of my nicely woven "I'm just an American" storyline are starting to split.

Bryce reaches out, a virtual hug. Gently he says, "You also don't want to leave yourself in a purgatory of perceived affront. Just ask him."

So I did. But by then, two weeks later, my indignation had waned, a flamethrower to a candle. I'm ashamed to say I didn't prosecute my case, ask all my questions, wait expectantly as a thinly veiled accusation—*What did you mean by that?*—twisted in the wind. Instead, on an audio call stripped of visual cues, I glossed over our conversation and didn't wait for his answer before plowing forward, dispassionately explaining why, "Oh, you were a manager?" might be offensive to some other, unnamed person of color who might be more sensitive than me. Because even though today's new paradigm is to confront systemic racism through uncomfortable conversations, these conversations make me uncomfortable too. All too often I've had to steel myself for a disingenuous counterargument, crudely disguised as an innocent question: *Why can't I call you Oriental? Why can't I call it the China virus? But the term "Chinese Wall" is used in law and business all the time! Why can't I say that?* All too often I've had to acquiesce and simply say, "Let's move on," instead of being honest and yelling, "Because it's racist!"

But on a committee where uncomfortable conversations are expected, and even encouraged, what kept me from pressing my colleague for an admission of bias? Or, less damning, a blind spot? Maybe I'm so grateful for my hard-won enfranchisement that I'm reluctant to confront white fragility.

Maybe I'm so assimilated that having a pointed argument on race feels too transgressive. Maybe "trying to be accommodating" is written into my lifeblood. Maybe I'm afraid of an awkward apology or, even worse, having to suffer a justification that doesn't ring true.

It's a familiar, dissonant roil, one I've only recently sought to understand. Cathy Park Hong's book, *Minor Feelings: An Asian American Reckoning*, describes the situation so well that I was overcome with both the shock of recognition (*that's me!*) and relief (*I'm not the only one*). She defines minor feelings as "the racialized range of emotions that are negative, dysphoric, and therefore untelegenic, built from the sediments of everyday racial experience and the irritant of having one's perception of reality constantly questioned or dismissed[7]." These are the feelings I've squelched all my life. As Hong describes, "Minor feelings are also the emotions we are accused of having when we decide to *be* difficult—in other words, when we decide to be honest. When minor feelings are finally externalized, they are interpreted as hostile, ungrateful, jealous, depressing, and belligerent, affects ascribed to racialized behavior that whites consider *out of line*." That's me, too. Success, in White America, demands restraint.

But by backing down, am I doing an even greater disservice? Because if I, who have some sense of enfranchisement, am reluctant to speak truthfully, how will those without that privilege have the courage to speak up and believe they will be heard?

If we can't talk about racism in a diversity committee, how will any other white space have a chance?

In early 2021, I revisited the topic of Asian Americans hitting the executive suite. How much progress have we made over the last twenty years? The answer is, not much[8,9]. In a broad 2020 analysis using EEOC National Workforce Data[10], Buck Gee and his team found that all racial minorities are underrepresented at the executive level relative to their professional levels, and the largest disparity was for Asian American men and women. Companies are eager to hire them, but not promote them. Since Asian American women are subject to both racial and gender gaps, essentially a "double whammy," they, along with Black women, are least likely to advance.

As I gaze into the gallery view of another weekly Zoom call, the other diversity committee members listen attentively while I rehearse my spiel for the annual members' meeting. I have three minutes to tell the boathouse membership about the Inclusion Project, as we've dubbed our initiative, and drum up support. I start with an apt sports reference, the Miami Marlins' recent selection of Kim Ng as their new General Manager. "This is personal, it means a lot to me," I say, and while my delivery has been honed by years of public speaking, my sincerity is genuine. "She's the first woman, the first Asian American woman, to be the GM of a major league baseball team. She was qualified ten years ago! The only icon of my era, the only positive representation we've had for almost a generation was," I pause dramatically, "Bruce Lee!" I lean in and stare straight into the camera. "Representation is important. If you don't see anyone who looks like you, in the media, in your workplace, and in your *boathouse*, you may feel you don't belong." In the glow of their computer screens, I can tell my cohorts appreciate my performance.

When I finish, there's quick feedback. "Nice job!" "Maybe shorten the committee introductions." "Make sure to emphasize adult recruitment." But then comes a comment that knocks me back a thousand paces. Rubbing his chin, the young guy says, almost tentatively, "So when you say 'we,' I'm not sure I know who you're talking about."

What? I hastily scan my notes for context, zero in on the ambiguous pronoun. *The only positive representation we've had for almost a generation…* My brow furrows. Why is that confusing? The answer hits me, and I feel an adrenaline surge. The dam between my internal and external reality buckles and bursts. I finally tackle it head on.

With my forefinger, I draw circles around my face. "Look!" I exclaim, "I'm not white!"

It's a pathetic laugh, but he laughs. Then, to my utter surprise he counters with, "But will the audience know what you mean?"

There it is again: the curse of the almost-white. Not elevated enough to be given equal power, not subjugated enough to be seen. Do I really have to preface a personal statement about representation with, "As an Asian American…"? Like the optical illusion where you see either a beautiful young woman or a kerchiefed old hag, unconscious bias shows you what you expect to see. Right now, I'm white in the boathouse. Weeks ago, I was an unlikely Asian American manager.

I bite my lip, tamp down my incredulity. I remind myself to keep this light: humor's a better teacher than humiliation. I paste on a broad smile as I stare wild-eyed into the camera, loudly proclaiming, "I'll be on *Zoom*! They can see my *face*! And my *name*!"

"Oh! Okay." He looks away. He doesn't sound convinced. My heart sinks. *He doesn't understand me!* Then a resigned sigh, with its corollary thought. *I'm getting nowhere. I might as well quit.*

But wait. Can there be another explanation? Am I so layered with oppression tokens that he doesn't want to presume which one I'm referring to? By invoking Kim Ng, I've surfaced at least three: Asian American female manager in a male-dominated profession. By asking for clarification, is he actually respecting my intersectionality and giving voice to *me*? Doing the *right* thing?

Damn. My unconscious bias is showing.

In the world I was raised in, there was no such thing as an anti-racist. The only two options were racist and not racist. On a personal and practical level, that binary was useful in safeguarding myself from harm. But that binary never imagined a change in paradigm, never imagined allies who actively work against systemic racism. Layer on progressive ideas of intersectionality—the mosaics of identity—and this is the nuanced worldview I've come to respect in Bryce. And, I wryly note, that's *perhaps* being exhibited by this young guy leading the diversity committee. Should he get the benefit of the doubt?

Something in our exchange reminds me of one of my favorite cartoons from Gary Larson's *The Far Side*. I stifle a laugh and magically my mood lifts. The first frame, labeled "What we say to dogs," features a man pointing his finger accusingly at his dog Ginger, who sits with perked ears as he repeats her name and berates her for getting into the garbage. In the second frame, the exact same graphic is labeled "What they hear," and the man's speech bubble is filled only with "*blah blah* Ginger *blah blah blah* Ginger."

This failure of words reminds me that communication's rarely perfect. Even with a speaker who's precise about word selection and careful with tone, the receiver, no matter who they are, interprets the message through the lens of personal experience and unconscious bias. Divining intent, especially with a skeptical ear, makes communication even more fraught. Add to that a potentially charged topic, and no wonder it's hard to have a civil conversation, much less reach a common understanding, on issues like race and diversity.

Now I have a deeper appreciation for this *Far Side* cartoon, for the genius of Gary Larson. We've all been recipients of messages we don't fully understand. The premise of the cartoon catches us at a key inflection point, the breath of a moment when a significant change may occur.

Notes

1. Ben L Erdreich, Antonio C Amador, and Beth S Slavet, "Fair and Equitable Treatment: A Progress Report on Minority Employment in the Federal Government. A Special Study. A Report to the President and Congress of the United States." (U.S. Merit Systems Protection Board, 1998), https://www.mspb.gov/studies/studies/Fair_and_Equitable_Treatment_A_Progress_Report_on_Minority_Employment_in_the_Federal_Government_253658.pdf.

2. Mike Swift, "Why Haven't Asians Scaled Corporate Heights?," *Seattle Times*, June 1, 2009.

3. Buck Gee and Wes Hom, "The Failure of Asian Success in the Bay Area: Asians as Corporate Executive Leaders," *Ascend Foundation*, March 28, 2009.

4. Asian American Executive Program (Stanford Graduate School of Business, n.d.), https://www.gsb.stanford.edu/exec-ed/programs/asian-american-executive-program.

5. Chinese Exclusion Act of 1882, Pub. L. No. 47–126, 22 Stat. 58, Chap. 126 (1882).

6. Geary Act of 1892, Pub. L. No. 52–60, 27 Stat. 25 (1892).

7. Cathy Park Hong, *Minor Feelings: An Asian American Reckoning* (New York: One World, 2021).

8. Buck Gee and Denise Peck, "Asian Americans Are the Least Likely Group in the U.S to Be Promoted to Management," *Harvard Business Review*, May 31, 2018.

9. Buck Gee and Denise Peck, "The Illusion of Asian Success: Scant Progress for Minorities in Cracking the Glass Ceiling from 2007–2015," *Ascend Foundation*, 2015.

10. Buck Gee, Tina Kim, and Denise Peck, "Race, Gender & the Double Glass Ceiling: An Analysis of EEOC National Workforce Data," *Ascend Leadership Foundation*, December 2020, https://www.ascendleadershipfoundation.org/research/race-gender-double-glass-ceiling.

Genesis
Erin Wilson

This I is curious
This I is smelling
This I is all nose
This nose pushes forth to part the space to know it
This I says "moon"
This I says "mine"
This I says "day" and "yes"
This I says "night," always, always
This I has legs and licks them
This licking is I
These legs traverse days in two scissors and a kick
These legs disturb moon like water
These legs are sticks of night
There is gnawing

*

Heard through night—a sound
The curious I moves forward
Night—over pewter—a sound again
A quickening of this I
A translocation as night thickens in
These sticks fall from drum of moon, two jouncing sticks of neon
This I cowers
This I closes eyes
     like pearl, like pearl, like pearl, wishing for tomorrow

*

This I is peppy
This I is ass of dog, dumb head of running rooster
This I is indomitable
This I is new day, principle revolution
Fetch crown, "I" crows I
"I king and I head remains!"
The flash from axe is bagatelle
This I bags it and wears it from I's belt

*

I struts
I struts and struts—is strutting
Struts and struts, tugging leaf tips—is tugging
Spring be I, behold nipples
Summer be I, behold pubis
Autumn be I, crack knuckles
Struts and struts, knowing knobby oak-gnarled peakness
Winter be I, contracted foreknowledge of enormous
Struts and struts, strutting and tugging, accounting kindling
Table be I
Flooring be I
Door frame be I
I reflected in doorknob—open
Behold vast reflection
World be I!

    [Sudden blindness with sight]

*

Become—a kick in I

I wrinkled

Become—a stain in I

I jaundiced

Band of world pushes back from I's pushing, pushing

I bounces

I stills on I's ass
I startled

I tests I's fingers
I startled

I tests I's eyesight
I startled

I wipes dust from I's eyes
I leaking

I fractured
Through I, world begins pouring in

*

I wrenches floorboards, starts pounding
    [Streaming kaleidoscope of crisps and colours]

I grabs at day and night and moon and bungs for fillers
    [Fleeting time in discombobulated refrains]

Crown goes to hole
Ass goes to forehead

Nipples point to hole, pubis pounds and pounds it
Seasons are flushing, are flushing, flushing
Spindly chaos spirals over hole and I is and I is and I
Bagatelle spins like golden rings and flushes out through hole
And Hole is I and I is black ellipses blink of wholeness

No accounting could have foretold the vastness of the nothing to follow such I.

Leaving Boystown
Mary Lynn Reed

Theo spun me around in the barber's chair, fingers pressing his lips. I'd asked for a "high and tight" crew cut and he didn't hold back. Displaying me like a prize, he yelled, "Look at this amazing boy I've created!"

No one cared. This was Northalsted, Chicago, and the place was full of smooth, real, beautiful boys. Through the mirror, I gave Theo my playful seductive glare. He fanned himself, and said, "Jesus, Dean, have mercy on me—"

I laughed, shifted my legs. Even with shoulder-length hair I was sometimes Sir'ed by the slightly distracted. I didn't mind. What unnerved me were the second glances, catching the fullness of my chest. Their embarrassment, and in the wrong place, anger. There were a lot of places where a girl with a crew cut could get her head bashed in.

Theo and I grew up together in Charleston. He let me crash on his sofa my first term at Northwestern, before the professor I'd come to work with found funding for me. Even after the money came in, it was hard to give up the proximity of Theo's sofa to the Boystown club scene. Lesbian bars didn't do a thing for me but I dug the flashing lights and hard-throbbing techno of Boystown.

"How's the love life?" I asked Theo.

He swept my hair into a pile, shook his head. "Richard studies too much but when he's a doctor it'll be worth it, I guess. Dustin is hot, hot, per usual. Keeps me sane."

"They still like each other?"

"Bizarre, isn't it?" He winked. "This ain't South Carolina, darlin'. We in Boystown, and we likes it!"

I was studying engineering back then. Had a knack for mechanical things. Dad was a tinkerer, Uncle Roy an electrician. I didn't know what I wanted to be but I was good at math and if I watched you take something apart, I could put it back together. Fast. Mom was determined I leave South Carolina with an education, and she had a little money tucked away that she never let Dad touch. So I went to Clemson, studied Mechanical Engineering.

Far back as I remember it seemed pre-determined that I would leave home, as if Mom always knew there was someplace else I ought to be. Grad school in a big, northern city seemed a fine alternative to an entry-level desk job in the hell-fire heat and blue-collar desperation of my childhood.

One night I was sipping warm beer out of a plastic cup at a campus party, found myself talking to Barb Wincheski, wife of Professor Peter Wincheski, Chair of the Department of Electrical Engineering. Barb owned an art gallery on Michigan Avenue. Her hands were well-manicured, nails painted bright pink, but she knew how to blend with the college crowd. Her Chuck Taylors color-matched her turtleneck and blazer.
  "I'm a bit of a shutterbug," I told her.
  She raised an eyebrow. "Your look is striking. Ever do self-portraits?"
  I fanned my exposed scalp, laughed. "I prefer the view from behind the lens—looking at others."
  I visited her gallery, took her to lunch.
  She loved the ballet, though she'd never danced.
  "Pose for me," I said, and we wound up naked in my apartment, camera never coming out of the case.
  Eventually, I did photograph Barb. Fully clothed, and in her element. She hired me to take a series of candid shots on the opening night of a post-modern neoclassical exhibit that left me a little dizzy.
  "What do you think?" she asked, delicately juggling a martini and her iPhone with one hand, her other grasping my arm.
  "I dig the symmetry," I said, enjoying the way she sidled in beside me.
  "Anything else?" She took a long sip of the martini.
  "Professor coming tonight?"
  "He hates art." She released my arm, and slid swiftly back to her clientele.
  I wasn't an event photographer, but I did my best. When I culled through the night's shots and presented my selections, Barb said I had a unique perspective.
  "It's complex," she said. "What you focus on—where your eye lingers."
  She wanted to see my independent work.
  "What are the subjects you return to, again and again?" she asked.
  "Underneath the El trains," I told her. "The shadows, the steel. It's like living under a geometric sky. I have hundreds of those shots."
  We were on the futon in my apartment. She was wearing one of my large tee shirts and nothing else. I was in my boxers.
  "Show me," she said.
  I pulled out my laptop, started a slideshow.

She had a regular buyer who loved gritty photos of the city. She asked if I made my own prints, if I'd ever sold anything. I was shocked and I guess it showed.

"It's okay," she said, her lips finding my collarbone, my shoulder. "I bet I can sell your work. If you're interested."

And sell it, she did. She took my images, had them professionally printed and framed, and sold five of them for five grand. I was in my Optimization of Engineering Design class when she texted and told me. I gasped and the girl next to me reached out to make sure I was okay, that no one had died or been hit by a car.

"No," I whispered. "My girlfriend is freakin' amazing."

That wasn't the only surprise Barb had in store for me.

"I'm leaving Peter," she said over pink cocktails at The North End.

I was so high on her sale of my photographs I almost missed what she said. The DJ had just kicked up the volume on the house beat, moving the bar's pace from Happy Hour to Evening Jam. Barb was looking past me, watching the boys trickle onto the dance floor.

"I'm sorry, I think you said—"

"I'm leaving him," she said again, turning and looking me straight in the eye.

"He's the Chair of the Department—"

Barb laughed. "And I'm the Queen of England. What the hell?"

"I don't know why I said that. It was the first thing that popped into my mind," I said.

She downed her little pink cocktail and pulled me onto the dance floor. We danced until closing, then went back to my place and fucked until dawn.

Turned out Professor Wincheski's marriage had been on the skids long before I came to town, but I still fell out of favor rather quickly in the Department of Electrical Engineering. Luckily I wasn't in that department but professors gossip worse than teenage girls. It didn't take long for the faculty on the Mechanical side to begin looking at me askew as well. It's not like I had been blazing a trail to academic glory before I met Barb. I was holding my own. I could have made it to a doctorate, if my energy had stayed focused in that direction. But once she'd sold a few of my photographs, a path I'd never let myself imagine opened up.

As soon as the divorce papers were served, I moved into Barb's apartment in the city. I bought a new camera with the money from that first sale, and took an official leave of absence from Northwestern.

"I can't keep your funding on hold," my advisor said. "Grants don't work that way."

His dusty office was full of textbooks and antique mechanical gadgets. The ridge in his forehead deepened with concern. He was a decent man but when I looked at his life, surrounded by dusty, old things, it didn't have the same magnetism of the crisp, clean lines in Barb's gallery downtown.

"I know it's a risk," I said. "But I want to take it."

It felt like leaping without a net. Except there was Barb, holding a net. She was smart and successful. She knew the art world, and she believed in me. I didn't know how to explain it to my professors, let alone my family back home in South Carolina. But quitting school didn't feel like a risk at all. My gut told me it was right.

I went to see Theo before I turned the paperwork in. My gut wanted some back-up. The barber shop was packed that day. So many gorgeous men, even I almost swooned when I walked in.

"You don't want me to tell you what to do," Theo said, dusting hair off a hunky blond's shoulders.

I sat on a stool tucked beside his station. I kept trying to spin it but it was solid, not a swivel.

"Just tell me I'm not crazy," I said.

Theo raised an eyebrow. "Sweetheart, we both know you're crazy as hell."

I kicked at the base of the stool. I really wanted that damn thing to spin.

"How's Dustin doing?" I said. "Is he working?"

"He got a commercial!" Theo said. "It's good pay."

Dustin did improv and stand-up comedy and was always at an audition.

"It's not crazy to be a photographer, right? I don't have to be a gallery artist. I could get a job at the Tribune. Or the police department—I could shoot crime scenes."

"Seriously, that's where your mind goes?" Theo said.

The hunky blond in Theo's chair turned to me. He was older than I'd realized. Forty or so. He must have been a bodybuilder at some point. "You're too young for this much angst, kid. If you want it, do it. It doesn't have to be your whole life. It's just the next thing on your list."

He had kind eyes. I smiled at him, and said, "Thanks."

I jumped off the stool, kissed Theo on the cheek.

That first year with Barb was a frenzy of "new life." I explored the city with my camera, seeking new angles and perspectives, searching for just the right light to shoot my favorite spots. I took some classes. Film and darkroom techniques. Digital, too. I joked that I had to quit school in order to learn all the things I wanted to learn.

Barb also threw herself into her new passion—being the best lesbian possible. She had plenty of gay male friends from the art world but now that she was with me, she set out to educate herself on all things women-loving-women. She went to the Women & Children First bookstore, walked right up to the counter, and said: "I'm a late-blooming lesbian and need a reading list to get me up-to-speed." She came home with a box full of books and devoured them all.

The one thing Barb said she missed from her professor's wife days were dinner parties. So one Saturday night we invited Theo, Richard, Dustin, and a lesbian couple Barb befriended at the gym over for homemade gnocchi and meatballs. Lisa and Jamie Hunt-Waters were a Chicago power couple, for sure. Lawyer and financial analyst, respectively. Barb was an art dealer, after all, and wealthy friends made fantastic customers. I hadn't met Lisa and Jamie yet but I knew I was supposed to make a favorable impression. Barb dressed me up in a white cotton button-down and a pair of leather wingtips for the evening. I went along without complaint. Didn't look half-bad, actually.

Barb worked all afternoon on the gnocchi, from a recipe she'd learned at a cooking class in Tuscany. "Learning to cook was the highlight of many vacations with the old Professor," Barb said.

"Worse things have come from marriage," Richard said, sneaking a taste of the sauce in the kitchen.

My contribution to the party was a playlist of downbeat ambient electronica, and chic little twinkle lights strung just under the crown molding throughout the dining room and den. Theo gave me a thumbs up on both, and the Hunt-Waters power couple didn't balk when they arrived, so I called it a success.

I passed around mini hors d'oeuvres. Dustin and Theo held hands, chatting with finance guru Jamie, who smiled a lot and didn't say much.

"What are you photographing these days, Dean?" Dustin asked.

"Train tracks," I said. "Intersections, in particular."

Richard swooped in. "Above ground?" he asked.

"No more under-shots of the El?" Theo asked. "You've graduated from bottom to top?"

Dustin nudged Theo's arm. "Just like you, dear—"

Theo's face flushed.

"A-ha!" I said. "Tell me more—"

Jamie slipped away, made her way back to Lisa's side.

Barb set the last serving plate on the dining room table, called us for dinner.

Richard and Dustin and Theo sat on one side of the table, Richard in the middle. I was at the far end, nudge-distance from Theo. Lisa and Jamie took up the other side, with Barb in the host seat, a fast dash back to the kitchen.

"What did I miss while I was in the kitchen?" Barb asked.

"Dean was telling us about shooting train tracks," Theo said.

"Intersections," I said.

"They're fabulous," Barb said. "Dean's work is progressing so rapidly. I can't wait to do a full show. It'll take Chicago by storm!"

"I'd love to see," Lisa, the lesbian lawyer said. She was a firmly built woman, with great posture. Clearly the gym fanatic.

Jamie was softer and quieter, her smile designed to conceal.

"You should give Lisa and Jamie a preview in your studio," Barb said. "After dinner."

My studio was a converted loft bedroom at the back of the apartment with a tricked-out computer and massive monitor for touching up digital images. I didn't usually let anyone back there and Barb knew it. I shot her a look, across the table. She smiled.

"I've been reading this remarkable book," Barb said.

Grateful for the change of subject, I grabbed a roll from the basket in the center of the table.

"It's a memoir of a female-to-male transsexual. Very thought-provoking," Barb said.

"See a lot of that in Boystown these days," Richard said, sipping his wine.

"Barb reads a lot of books," I said. "I think she's studying up for Queer Jeopardy."

Jamie smiled.

"I dated a drag queen once," Dustin said. "Hardest top I ever knew!"

Barb looked displeased. She tossed her head to the side, angled her commentary toward Lisa and Jamie. "The description of the writer's gender dysphoria—feeling out of sync with your own body—it got to me," she said. "Made me think hard about what it means to be a woman. Or a man."

"I think it's sad," Lisa said. "All the butch dykes are disappearing, replaced by beards and hairy chests."

Richard touched his facial hair, and Lisa quickly added, "No offense."

"None taken."

"Besides that, there are so many different labels now. Non-binary, pansexual, omnisexual, an entire spectrum of asexuality. I can't keep up. Makes me feel so old," Lisa said.

"The gnocchi is really fantastic," I said. "Isn't it?"

Richard and Dustin moaned, nodding their agreement. Forks clanked against plates, scooping pasta with abandon.

"Richard's about to start an internship at Northwestern Memorial," I said.

Barb gripped the table, and said, "Congratulations, Richard. That's wonderful. But Dean, I was talking about this book. About transsexuality. Why are you changing the subject? Does it make you uncomfortable?"

Theo laid his hand on my knee under the table. I didn't realize my whole body had tensed into a tight coil until he touched me. There was a decade's difference between my age and Barb's. I rarely thought about it, until it lit up the room like a neon sign. She looked at me like a child.

"When did you stop using your girl name?" Barb continued. "When did you become Dean, and not Robin?"

The room fell quiet, except for the slow lounge groove still playing softly from the Bose.

I put my fork and knife down gently, pushed back from the table.

Theo jumped in, and said, "Eighth grade. We were thirteen and had just watched *Rebel Without A Cause*. I said, *I'm gonna call you Dean*. It just stuck. She was that cool. Then, and now."

Everyone's eyes were on me. I held Theo's gaze, counting silently in my head.

Barb had never mentioned this book to me, or asked me these questions when we were alone. She waited until she had an audience. Until I couldn't deflect the interrogation. And that's what it was. She'd been saving it up for awhile. Little things that hadn't made any sense before became clear. She'd been carefully avoiding gendered pronouns for months. Every time she referred to me to anyone, I was "Dean," never "she," "he," not even "them."

Barb stared at me across the long table. "So you found your true self at thirteen," she said. "Did your parents call you Dean after that?"

"My true self?" I said.

Theo turned to Richard, then Richard to Dustin.

"We're all unique, I think," Jamie said, the sound of her voice startling everyone. She hadn't spoken more than a single word all night. But now she said, boldly, "Who we love. Who we are. How we present ourselves to the world. How can it be defined in a few words? Or even a name. We're just ourselves, I think."

"Right," I said. "That's right."

"But it's also about honesty," Barb said. "We should be honest about who we are, shouldn't we? At least to ourselves."

I was masculine, yes. Never felt comfortable in women's clothes. My voice was thick and heavy (sultry, some women said), my jaw square. But what gives someone the right to take those facts and proclaim I'm not in the right body? Or that I'm not being honest about who I am? I was working myself up to saying all that out loud, when Richard cleared his throat, and stood up.

"I'm thirsty, that's what I am. More wine, anyone?" he said.

There was a collective exhale. Everyone shifted and turned.

Barb got up to clear the dinner plates. I opened another bottle of wine. Two hours later, they were all gone. I sat in my studio with the lights out until the apartment was quiet, and I knew Barb was asleep. I texted Theo to find out which club they'd gone to, joined them for a few hours of dancing before the blinding lights switched on at four a.m. We ended up at the all-night diner.

Theo and Richard and Dustin. The three of them were about as different as three gay men could be, yet together, they just made sense. And they were smart enough not to sit around and try to dissect why it worked, or what it all meant, or to throw a lot of bullshit labels on it to try to make other people comfortable.

"You okay?" Theo asked.

"Never better," I said. I was drenched in sweat from the dancing and the still air of the diner.

"Hang in there," Richard said. "Crazy as that shit was, I think that woman loves you. In her own, ex-professor's-wife-Michigan-Ave-art-dealer kind of way."

I laughed.

Dustin finished off a full stack of pancakes and two orders of bacon, and said, "Man, I wish we had some more of that gnocchi. That stuff was de-lish."

We spent another hour talking about Richard's internship and Dustin's commercial. All the things that would have made great dinner party conversation with the Hunt-Waters couple, if Barb hadn't hijacked the night for her gender identity detective mission.

I bought some danish and coffee to go, took it home. Put the stuff on a little silver tray and brought it to the bedroom. When I opened the door, Barb was sitting straight up, wide awake.

"Have fun with the boys?" she said.

I put the tray over her legs, and kissed her. "I brought you breakfast."

"Mmm-hmm." She carefully moved the tray off the bed, pulled me down on top of her. We moved together, slowly at first. Kissing. Rhythm picked up, and I reached into the side table.

"Why?" she said.

Fourteen Hills

I stopped, looked at her. "Why what?"

"Why wouldn't you answer my questions last night? Why were you so uncomfortable?"

"Why'd you wait to ask in the middle of your dinner party?"

She pushed me off. "I don't know. Maybe it freaks me out, too. Reading that book, it made me wonder. Whether you might be in some kind of gender crisis."

"Crisis? You know how that sounds, right?"

"Do your parents call you Dean? Why don't I know the answer to that question? Have you ever talked to a therapist? If you won't talk to me—"

"I'm quiet, that's all. Why does it matter what name my mom and dad call me? I like boys clothes and I like to fuck women. So what? I don't need a goddamned shrink. Is this even about me? Maybe you're in crisis? What do your books say about that?"

I'd moved to the dresser, started shoving clothes into a duffle bag.

"That's not fair," she said. "I love you, you little shit. Can't you see I want you to be happy?"

Outside of family, no woman had ever said she'd loved me before that. Leave it to Barb to declare it in the middle of a fight.

"I need to clear my head," I said.

She sat on the side of the bed, head in her hands.

"I'm gonna go up to Evanston, get my Toyota out of storage, and take a drive," I said.

"Where are you going?"

I sat down beside her, took a deep breath.

"It took a while but yes, my parents do call me Dean. It's a nickname. That's all. I'm not in a crisis. Whatever the hell that means. I'm just going to take a drive. I'll shoot wildflowers on the side of the road and I'll think about what you're saying. Okay? I'll think about all of it. I just need to clear my head."

She exhaled, sat up straighter. "Lisa texted me this morning. She wants three of the pieces you showed her last night. You've got real talent, Dean. No matter what else happens, know that I can sell your work. Okay? Know that I will do that for you, no matter what."

I kissed Barb on the forehead, put a couple more T-shirts into my bag, and left.

I stopped at the barber shop on my way out of town. Theo gave me a fresh cut and an extra long hug. He walked out to the car with me.

"I don't know about this backroads crap," he said. "There are a lot of Southern accents between here and Miami. What's wrong with the Interstate? You like to drive fast."

"Not this time. Everything's a blur from the Interstate. Barb is a pain in the ass but she might be right about a few things. Too much of my short life has already been a blur. I should move slower for a while, pay attention to the details. If I'm going to be an artist, I should see more of the world—and maybe, understand more about myself."

Theo squeezed my hand. "All right, you be safe. Boystown to South Beach. It's a gay pilgrimage, Baby... take me with you. I swear, I'll be very quiet."

I laughed, rolled the windows down in the Toyota. A pair of beautiful men holding hands passed by, smiling. I took a deep breath and pulled away, heading south on Halsted.

Catfish
Nathan Kosta

archival pigment print
40" × 52"

Systematic Theology
Don Swartzentruber

watercolor, ink, and gouache on bristol paper
11" × 15"

Hand of God
Stefan Karlsson

Of course I noticed how my aunt, who spoke
haltingly, savored reciting her Hail Marys, words she knew
by heart, but when I saw how quickly she turned

to cursing, frustrated that her tongue, touched
by Broca's aphasia from a stroke, trailed behind
her solemn thoughts, and how she turned against

her parents—my grandparents who took care
of her—seemingly randomly, seething
till they talked her down and returned

her rosary, its familiar beads and broken
spaces, its measured pauses, to her trembling hands,
I hardly tried to understand why we gave thanks

to the God who let her suffer. My family grows taut
with faith, I thought. But now I see how piety
makes people pliant to chance, the way my grandfather

places all in the Hand of God, Hand that strokes
his back and leaves it brimming—as the CAT scan
says plain—with cancer. Hand, your shadow grows

denser, darkness spreading as you plummet
from your golden armrest like an anvil falling
from the sky that I looked to as a boy, ever faithful

as my pipsqueak prayers got whack-a-moled. Hand,
peel me off the floor where I'm flattened,
unsquish me, squeeze the last life from my splatted

spirit; Hand, I don't want to be pinned
to the wall to hang, wings spread, another beautiful
specimen. My aunt's frontal lobe

pressed deep into the earth, my grandfather's spine
wrung out like a rag till nothing is left
but devotion. The bells ring for you and I join hands

with them one last time. Hand, don't touch me.

The Devil's Chord
Candice Wuehle

～

The pain doctor's office was covered in laminate. Posters that featured bodies and even parts of bodies, isolated, which were neither clinical nor cartoonish in their depiction. They occupied the vague space of symbol, smooth lines abstracted into recognizable shapes. Three zigged lightning bolts shooting from the neck. A transparent swarm poised over the low back.

Although the messages were opaque, their meaning was obvious if you spoke what the pain doctor termed the language of pain.

The pain doctor was always so busy because there was so much pain in the world that it pained him that I could not be quicker, clearer, when explaining my own pain. Why, his frown asked, couldn't I just learn the language? Why, he wondered, couldn't a woman like me just accept she was in a new country? Every few months I came in and sat my papered ass on his papered table and insisted on speaking English. I acted like a tourist, entitled to my ignorance, dependent on him, the pain doctor, for help with simple tasks: moving, working, thinking. Tasks I could accomplish if only I would learn it. The language of pain.

"How are we feeling today?" This was his way of inviting me to the country. We were a we, countryman and countrywoman.

"Good," I responded. I flashed, then, to a compendium of CDs and workbooks my mother had given me as a child so I could learn to speak Latin, the original language. The courses were taught by Muzzy, a monster the color of a surgical gown, and his friends, cartoon royals outfitted in '70s tones: burnt orange, straw, gourd. When Muzzy asked a question, I responded with a specific answer; a ventriloquization achieved easily since Muzzy had only taught me one response.

The pain doctor was not so lucky. I was supposed to respond with one of the letters on his chart. It was a joke chart, but also I was supposed to take it seriously. It said things like A = might be a hangnail or Q = vampire bite? "Good" was not charted.

The pain doctor, with exertion, tapped a zombie crawling out of a grave—Y. "How are we feeling *on the chart?*"

"Oh," I said, as if now I understood, "X."

He nodded sympathetically. W = dead.

"What seems to be our problem?"

"It 'seems' 'our' thighs are burning, but there are no burns." The pain doctor opened his mouth to speak but I persisted. "The muscles in my back feel stretched, like I'm on the rack. And my hands," I held them up, "clench in, like claws. But I can't feel the top of my right hand at all. It's numb, like ice."

Metaphor was the one linguistic strategy the pain doctor and I agreed on. Neither of us knew how to convey what was happening directly.

Normally the pain doctor responded with his own metaphors, transmissions so meager they barely counted. "It's like," he struggled to think what my pain was like, "it's like you can't catch a break, huh?"

Yes, I would agree. I couldn't catch one.

That month, though, I must have gone too far when I said X. Of course that was too far—X was after dead, barely in the alphabet. That month the pain doctor didn't give me a figure of speech and a renewed prescription at all. He gave me two names. One was for a physical therapist and the other was my diagnosis.

It was my own fault for breaking our covenant. For pointing to the speechless place where the answers came back distorted, removed from the world of known things.

People who named things believed they understood those things. Before the pain doctor, I'd tried a yoga teacher who had a sobriquet for everything—postures, imaginary places in the body, types of breathing. She even had a name for not looking too closely at anything, for a vague stare: *drishti*.

The teacher wore a loose shirt emblazoned with a jeweled elephant. It glittered and glared as she made prayer hands and other mudra. Like me, it rolled its eyes when she translated an ornately pronounced Sanskrit phrase into English.

Viparita Kurani, she intoned. *Legs up the wall.*

I always wished she'd do it in reverse—I had to wait for the English translation every time, which caused a kind of latency.

Adho mukha svanasana. Everyone else floated into a formation of downward facing Vs.

At this point, a freak of pain would slice through a muscle deep inside the fleshy mound between my buttock and hip, a pushing agony about the size of an entire newspaper, crumpled. As I aimed my anus toward the sky, I felt the crease of my right leg fold in deep and sudden. Between my legs, I made eye contact with the disco elephant and saw the future. Not with my third eye, but with whatever the opposite of that eye is.

After that, I went to the pain doctor and after the pain doctor told me to go to the physical therapist I went home and put my computer on my lap—it was hot, the fan breathing *ujjayi* like the yoga teacher, its space black bottom shooting radiant heat directly into my thighs—and curled myself towards the screen like a penitent. My hands clawed the keys and I pictured Muzzy, his monstrous insistence on repetition. *This world is full of horrors*, I thought as I genuflected to Outlook.

Without the renewed pain prescription, though, it quickly became impossible to keep asking the laptop for answers. Both because my fingers betrayed me, curling in towards my wrists like I was, what, a wraith? No, a martyr. On a pyre. Also because everything was dull without the medication. My search queries just kept returning me to myself. This must be what Joan of Arc felt like, I thought. Praying all the time and never getting any answers.

I pushed the laptop away and tried to find a new position.

Standing bent me forward at the waist and backwards at the neck. Like a Z. You know, they're thinking of removing that letter entirely. Replacing it with something more obvious. Like X.

For a while, I paced and felt my secret muscles recoil, wither, until my pelvic bowl titled and splashed like a tipped cauldron. My feet thumped a hitched drag anyone would fear to hear in a dark alley, the left pounding and the right hovering.

Finally, I leaned against the wall and my heavy left foot sucked into the carpet, pulling the rest of me down into what the yoga teacher had called *savasana*. Corpse pose.

Ignore her, the bedazzled pachyderm had advised and I *had* ignored her but now there I was, alone on my floor, the living dead. I stared at the ceiling and listened to my computer beckon from across the room. The muscles of my eyes, stuffed with blue laptop light, throbbed. My claws jerked to answer each ding emitted by my electronic overlord. In my third eye, I saw I had slunk to the floor in my true form: the Z shape.

Perhaps, also, my final form. Incorruptible as a saint or beati placed in one of those glass coffins. My thighs burned the laptop burn and I imagined the pain doctor visiting my entombed but perfectly preserved corpse.

How are we today? he would, for once, not say.

Finally, he would have to admit he had been wrong about the throb I had no name for in the muscle he claimed did not exist. Other saints, I knew, surrendered themselves well before death. The yoga teacher concurred. "Nirvana," she said, "isn't bliss like people think but actually a state beyond all states. A total removal from doing, from our internalized capitalism and the false sense of worth we believe comes from doing." The elephant had shimmered stoically.

Resigned, but also relieved, I closed my third eyelids and tried to feel nothing, to feel worthless. To be clear and holy as pure light, as crystal, as laminate. But almost immediately, my first eyelids flew open and I felt I had to tell the pain doctor one more thing while I was still of this world.

Squeezed as an accordion, I contorted into a smaller font so I could access my cell phone. The pain doctor was the last number dialed, so I needed click only once. Just as I moved to deploy the call, though, I realized I still had no idea what to say. No words to explain what was, for him, not yet there.

The body spoke in code. A series of encrypted sensations there was sometimes not yet language for: the bright, inarticulate shimmer of divine knowledge that requires a sacred guardian.

An image of Muzzy appeared before me then, a shadow at the edge of my mind slipping quick as a cryptid into the forest edge of my memory.

I clicked over to the App Store to look for Muzzy, but my search yielded nothing but a long list of language learning subscriptions that expected me to pay a monthly yield to learn another tongue in its entirety. I didn't need to be a master, though, just a messenger.

After all, I already knew the language of my own body. I just needed someone to impress it on the pain doctor, to make him feel it.

"To make him fucking feel it," I said, aloud.

As if summoned, a new app appeared in the store.

The mini squoval featured a simple black and white grid overlaid with four swirled red dots. No, not dots—fingerprints. Expanded, it became apparent that the logo for the nameless app was not a grid but a diagram of guitar strings depicting a specific finger placement.

I registered that the first sentence of the app's description was written in Latin before I bothered to read the Latin itself. I had already depressed the *download now* button when I comprehended: *Diabolus in Musica. Once banned by the church, this tritone chord was believed to inspire sinister sensations in all who heard its dissonance. Musicologists ascribe this reaction to the chord's unresolvability; its resistance to legibility. Because Diabolus in Musica cannot be produced by the human voice, songs sung in this chord are a clear indicator of possession.*

Heat from the phone pulsed into my palm. My wrist ached with the uncanny angle holding the device required. My thumb trembled as I clicked open the app, which at first seemed to be malfunctioning. It was nothing but a black screen, a lapse in digital time.

"Typical," I said to the screen and made to try Duolingo (an ad told me they had all sorts of experimental languages—Klingon, Elvish, possibly Pain), but just then the screen beamed a forked tongue, flicking. Beneath it, one word: *translating*.

Then, the chord map appeared and a low tone leaked from my phone. As if a dog responding to a whistle, my body jerked.

"Jesus Christ," I hissed. The reptilian tongue translated again, but this time the sensation was so intense my hand flew from the phone to the unnamed muscle deep inside. I could, for once, actually feel it spasm.

I kept speaking aloud despite the pain. No, because of it. My secret muscle responded so keenly to my translated speech that I actually lifted my shirt to look at it, to see it wriggling, and saw instead a jagged shape beneath my blouse. Little red welts springing forth, stamping my skin from the inside.

No, not welts—a letter.

A jagged Z, printed again and again from some interior typewriter.

I smiled, smug.

Now, I knew, the pain doctor would understand.

As I dragged myself toward the door, I thought of all the saints in their clear cases, suffering over messages others refused to receive. In the distance, my computer chimed like church bells.

Broken Sonnet for the American Schoolgirl
Mary Henn

Sunday: make up the couch,
lay a sheet over its face

to keep your mother's body

from staining
        it.   Monday: a school
              secretary announces the Pope is sick, code

for your teacher to turn off lights, lock
doors, pass a basket spilling with rosaries.

Pray your father won't come home. Hide.

Tuesday: help your mother bathe, watch
her naked and bruised, stitch after
stitch popping and dissolving while

fingers move along beads
to muffle the gunshot—a veil   over the black and blue of it.

Ode to a Makeshift Heroin Pipe
Mary Henn

∼

Construct
the empty Corona
      of muted cells and mock stars, of stolen
      brother. Recall what a child was
      made of, once unaware of.
           Rim the lip with

sugar,
watch residue
      crawl to the bottom, the circle
      where flame has gone—a glass space
           of forgotten birthday cake—

sliced open
palms reaching
      for lost crowns and crayons,
      hands full of blood and lighter and bone,
      and the sting of what does not burn
           after being set on fire.

Home Videos Tells Us Again
Mary Henn

He tucked into velvet-
upholstered chairs as we painted

pictures of girls in front of his
lime-tinted glasses, wide enough

to kill her frame by frame. Each brush
and stroke of the shoulder a glare

in the lens of a previous day, before
we knew what he had done.

The way he watched his daughter
before the car accident, her tanned legs

in short shorts and the end of April.
Her stillness, like rain pressed to glass

in his truck as he drove across country,
one hand on the wheel.

Rager
Ron Koertge

~

Kitty bungees her skateboard to her bike. Nic slides his into a backpack. Single-file on Speedway Avenue, then 6th Street more or less toward Picture Rocks but not really. The streets get narrow.

Little houses topped by swamp coolers sit side by side. People lounge on porches drinking beer and pop. Kids play badminton without a net.

Lights dangle from blue Palo Verde trees. One yard features a big, old Saguaro draped with fairy lights.

There's not many cars. Kitty rides right beside Nic. Asks, "Can you see yourself doing that?"

"What, decorating my cactus?"

They cruise past a duplex with two bright blue doors. Hear an argument from inside.

"Settled down," she says. "The same thing every night, same job next day."

"Maybe it's not like it looks."

"Yeah? I'll bet it's a lot like it looks. And talking about how things look, it looks to me like we're lost. I mean, you know where we're going, right?"

"Yep. Paloma Cielo."

"That place is farmsville, Nic."

"It's where the bash is."

"How'd you hear about it?"

"You're not the only one with an iPad."

Houses get further apart. More cars in the driveway. An RV. A boat. A three-bedroom every now and then. Then nothing but a glowing square at the edge of the desert. All glass in the front.

Nic points at the 7-Eleven. "We should score some snacks."

Kitty puts on her sunglasses. They're the only ones in the place. They fill up a little basket with chips and jerky. Oreos. Mountain Dew. Liters of it. Water.

Kitty says, "Don't get Jolly Rancher Gummies. They come with an 800 number that connects you directly to the nearest dentist."

The pimply clerk doesn't bother to take out his ear buds. He just nods to some secret music until it's time to sort things out. Then he asks,

"Where's the party?"

Nic points.

"Where out there?"

Kitty asks, "Do you skate?"

A headshake.

"It's that kind of party. Empty pool."

"Lots of girls?"

"Who knows." says Nic. "Probably."

Kitty says, "Give me your phone number. I'll send you some snaps."

"Seriously?"

"Front us this grub, yeah. For sure."

The clerk—his name tag says Dev—says, "I can't. There's cameras and stuff."

"Sure. I understand. You're being paid well and treated even better by an understanding employer who just wants the best for you."

"Okay, wait." Dev scribbles a number on a random receipt. Hands it to Kitty.

He inspects every bag and bottle. Pretends to tap on the register.

"Now give me ten bucks. I'll give it back at the party."

She says, "So see you at Paloma Cielo."

"Bullshit. Nobody lives there."

"Part of the point for a rager, wouldn't you think?"

"Okay, but where exactly?"

"You'll hear it."

"I close at ten."

"7-Ten," Kitty says. "Lacks the poetry of 7-Eleven. Those five original syllables could start a haiku."

"I had a gun in my face the other night. Guess how much they got. Forty-seven dollars. So I close at ten."

They glide into the darkness. The plastic bag of food knocks against the frame of his mountain bike.

"Are you really going to text him?" Nic asks.

"Dev? Sure, I might want to hook up after, have his baby, and argue every night."

They pause at the entrance to the subdivision. They stare at the huge sign beaten up by blowing sand and sun. A gigantic dove hovers over a smiling family.

Nic takes a still-cold can of Coke out of the bag, pops it open, hands it over.

"I have a hunch," Kitty says, "that this is the last courteous gesture I'll see all night from anybody."

She up-ends the red can, pounds down a lot if it. Belches. Nic finishes, drops the empty can in the bag.

"Pack it in," says Kitty. "Pack it out. Leave no trace."

"My dad said this place would never get built."

"He worked out here?"

"Talked to the developer who wanted to cut every corner."

"No way would your dad do that."

They meander through the ghostly streets where the toughest weeds in the world have a foothold. Candles flicker in a two-bedroom with a grinning skull on the garage and a hatchet buried in the door.

"Tell me this isn't the place, Nic."

"This isn't the place." He glides to a stop. "Listen."

Music or what passes for music. Lots of distortion. Funhouse shrieks. Death metal melodies.

The closer they get, the louder it gets. More kids standing around, showing up, leaving, pretending to leave. Waiting for something to happen. Anything.

Nic hides their bikes out past ATVs, dune buggies, Jeeps stripped down to the essentials and a Volvo or two, somebody's mom's station wagon.

They weave through full-on Mohawks, fauxhawks, shaved heads, tattoos, ponytails, fros. Girls in orange pants made from parachutes, orchid-colored hair, leather, raccoon eyes, torn tights, fishnets that are just shreds, emo boots with ten buckles.

At the door, a bare chested kid in leather pants that smell like road kill says, "*Cinco dolares.*"

Kitty asks, "Does that include the vegetarian buffet and a beverage of our choice?"

Nic opens his backpack, holds the skateboard aside. The doorman looks in, takes a handful of Slim Jims. Steps back.

Nic empties the backpack onto a counter where a hundred people have put out cigarettes. At the sound of all that crinkly cellophane, half a dozen kids look up from two ruined couches.

"Nic! Hey."

"Wilson. What's up?"

Wilson holds out a palm full of pills. "Want to get high?"

"Maybe after."

Wilson turns to Kitty, "How about you?"

"She doesn't want any, either," Nic says.

Kitty says, "He's insanely jealous. Better stop flirting with me."

Nic makes his way through what was once the living room. Smoke swirls around him—Marlboros, doobies, a fire pit somewhere close.

On a long table somebody arranged beer bottles in a V, like bowling pins. A bewildered turtle balances on the edge.

Nic knows Kitty is right behind him. Without even looking he hands over his board. "Be right back."

"I'll wait. And I'll be as faithful as Penelope."

Nic carries the turtle onto the patio and through a gate with no door. Ten yards later he's in the desert. Then another ten yards, watching his step. He takes a deep breath. Looks up at the stars.

On the way back, a girl as thin as an exclamation mark blocks his way. She's in shorts, flip-flops, a thrift store fur jacket with nothing or not much underneath it.

"I was gonna do that," she says. "Poor turtle." She holds out a damp-looking joint. Every fingernail has a little jewel in it. "Laura."

Nic politely takes a hit. "I was gonna go skate."

"Maybe I'll come watch."

Nic edges by her. He smells tobacco and patchouli.

Nic finds Kitty studying a wall almost black with graffiti. Layers of it. A kid he doesn't know has one arm around her. Leaning into her.

"Hey, Nic," she says. "I was just telling Victor Feldman here about some of the first graffiti ever. *Cueva de las Manos*. Argentina. Before Jesus even."

Victor holds out a bottle with something in it. "Want a drink?"

Kitty shakes her head. "I'm gonna hit the pool."

"No, hang on. One sip and all your troubles disappear."

Nic looks at Victor's grimy hand on Kitty's wrist. Looks at Victor.

The hand retreats. And then the rest of Victor.

"He was harmless," Kitty says.

"With his little ketamine cocktail?"

"Maybe. Probably not. Anyway, I would never cheat on you, break your heart, and drive you into the moors howling with grief."

"Good to know."

They check out the empty pool. Kids sit on the edge, legs dangling. Couples nuzzle each other, their Mohawks sparring. Skaters make a kind of line.

"Big crack at the bottom," Nic says. "By the drain."

"No worse than Locoville."

"Nic?"

They both turn. Tall guy. A tank top shows he's been to a gym. He's got a board with big wheels.

"Paul, remember? I skated at Locoville before it was Locoville. Don't tell me you're still there? Man, that place got hazardous fast."

Kitty says, "It's not that bad. And almost like a private club."

"I miss you guys. You can really skate. There's a bunch of toddlers at Diablo." He looks at Kitty. "My little sister reads your post every morning. She's impressed that I know you."

"Cool. Tell her thanks."

Paul nudges Nic with his board. "Is Goat Boy still at Locoville?"

"And Griff and Robster, yeah."

"Goat Boy gave me the creeps."

Kitty stops playing with the wheels of her deck and leans toward the pool. Nic and Paul drift that way, too. Through the double doors, not that there are doors, anymore. Some mobber scrawled *ABANDONAR TODA EXPERANZA* across the scarred header.

Laura drifts up, "Hey, Paul."

They hug agreeably.

Paul says, "You guys know each other? Kitty, Nic—"

"Nic and I bonded over *Gopheros agussizii*. Desert tortoise to you."

He and Paul and Laura follow Kitty, watch her get in line.

"Did you ever skate here?" Nic asks.

Paul nods. "Or someplace like it. I like the scene."

Mostly Nic sees skaters weaving around haplessly. Some frontside grinds, big air now and then and more not-so-big air. A slam that makes everybody wince. Then the limping away to inspect the damage.

"Whose place is this, anyway?" Laura asks.

"Who knows.," says Paul. "Probably some doofy who got behind on his house payments and just walked away."

Laura shakes her head. "It was nice once. People ate dinner out here. With candles probably. Fuck."

A couple of girls in bikini tops and cut offs pose where the diving board used to be. Kitty drops in, shoots under them, right up the side and into a hand plant. Totally vertical for two, maybe three, seconds

"Very nice," says Paul.

Laura tugs at Nic.

"In a minute."

Nic reads the concrete. Then takes his turn. Nothing fancy, but smooth. Apparently effortless. A run like that is sewing things together so the seams don't show.

He comes back panting a little. Laura takes his hand. His wrist actually. A little like he's under arrest.

She leads Nic down the hall. Into a room that has a microclimate all its own: Testosterone and heavy breathing and heat. Nic is surprised there's not water dripping from the ceiling.

Laura pushes him against the wall. Kisses him like they're about to be parted for years. Nic feels her everywhere. She's boney but pliable. He knows a door is opening and he can walk through if he wants to.

"Laura! Laura!"

She mutters, "Balls. Stay right here."

Nic waits a beat or two, picks up his board, makes his way down the hall, stepping over a kid in a tiara. Then past a guy whose cornrows are so tight they look painful.

He starts looking for Kitty. Finds her in what's left of the kitchen. Everything they brought has disappeared. There's half a pizza, though. Warm beer and soda.

Kitty asks, "Did you get up close and personal with that size zero worm-girl?"

"Sort of."

"Victor Feldman tried to feel me up. He won't do that again any time soon. Hang on a minute."

Nic watches her take a picture of a couple of girls making out by the picture window. She checks the phone number on that receipt. Sends. Says, "That'll make Dev close up early."

"It's past ten already. We should bounce."

Outside on the way to their bikes, they stop and watch two kids grunt and pound on each other.

Kitty leans into Nic, "Probably arguing about gender-neutral pronouns."

Nic asks, "Want to crash at my house?'

"I guess," Kitty says, "or we could be like Odysseus who said he wanted to go home, but he really didn't."

The Object World Is Small
Sean Cho A.

〜

Hypothesis:
science is metaphorical.

Really. Try to explain the distance from La Rinconada to Proxima Centauri
without comparing the space between the pepper grinder and your
salad fork. I am constantly disappointed with the limitations of the object world.
It's my problem that I never took a science class after AP physics so when you
say lightyear, and I try to change the topic to line breaks we
both need more context.

Last weekend my partner and I were waiting in line to board a boat
to go whale watching. A woman who looked like she could have been
my mother said, *jul seogo issnayo*. I needed more context, I needed to restart
my lifetime, stay in Busan, and learn the language is associated with my face.

Today I read online that for $10,000 geneticists can clone your dog
from a single hair or slobber sample. Taffy is getting old,

I carry him on the second half of walks
and I find this comforting. Engineers in "Industry" make

on average five times
as much as their counterparts
in academia.

Today an obscure literary journal paid me 50 dollars for a poem.

I need to write many more poems.
I wish they never made that movie about dogs going to heaven.

I want to write a poem for Taffy, and get it published on the same day he
leaves the world, so a few random strangers online can know some
guy with too-long hair is grieving normal sadness in an ordinary way.

I wonder if we'd like the same things again. I wonder if our friends
would recognize our scents, or our mangled hair. We want it to be dinner

time already, and I want to use the phrase "American" food.

The End of the Novel
Laura Ritland

At first, we tried to raise water
with our fists. The last chapter
had left us ropeless, hatless, blinking
a little stupidly in the honey-colored light

of a conclusion. The instructions
had been simple: be silent and procreate.
And so, despite our helplessness
or the way our skin refused the new sun,

we lifted our thin figures
from the fields' pages and set out
with our shadows before us.
Where we encountered nothing

but horizon, we set up camp. A ledge
between now and the ever-after
blessed us with shade, a crack
in the coda with spring water.

In time, the wide plains became
preplanned housing and our factories
circled the lakes. We invented holidays,
gasoline, paydays, and children, clocks

to stop the beat of eternity and wellfields
for glittering cities in the deserts.
We had our histories, now. We raised
water to our own lips. How impossible,

we sometimes thought, to think they
could be going on without us. We,
who had our own private and full lives,
growing wheat and killing animals.

Yet when great doors slammed in the sky
we half-hoped they would come back for us.
They never did, but we loved that story.
We loved it for dear life.

Crimes Against the Peace of the State

Sean Maschmann

∽

T&H Frozen Foods was nestled in a light industrial estate on Esquimalt Road, close enough to the ocean to smell the salt on the air. It shared the little complex with a dozen other businesses in two identical buildings separated by a parking lot. Daybreak Tofu was across the lot. There was a pet food manufacturer that took up two adjacent units. There was also a small printer at the end of the lot on the same side as us, next to the endless blackberry bushes and the Dayliner tracks.

And there was T&H Frozen Foods: the largest maker and distributor of sausage rolls to Vancouver Island, as well as Vancouver and the Fraser Valley.

Making all of those thousands of sausage rolls only took a crew of three. One of these was the owner, a gruff but kind man in his mid-fifties from Poland named Trofim. He had started T&H ten years earlier with a partner he eventually bought out: the mysterious 'H.'

I had graduated from Esquimalt High in June of 1987. My grades were terrible and I didn't end up going to UVic with most of my friends. I moved out and got a job at T&H the month after I graduated.

And there was Dylan, tall, skinny, and a few years older than me. His Adam's apple was massive and his hair was already thinning out. He had started right after graduating too. He knew everything about the process, and on the one or two days Trofim couldn't be around, Dylan took over. We became friendly enough that we would drive to the A&W up on Esquimalt Road in his blue Skylark with The Eagles or Tom Petty blaring.

At first, I was enthralled by the process of constructing sausage rolls. The rolling of the dough was a revelation. We used a giant Hobart machine and sent the dough through in ten-kilo batches to be flattened, oiled, and re-flattened until it reached 32 layers of tissue-thin pastry, which we would then place on a twenty-foot-long table like a massive blanket. The rolling machine was massive, gleaming. It was frightening and beautiful at once.

As the new guy, I had to mix the meat every morning. We used a pork-beef mix, but also made some straight beef rolls for the kosher and halal markets. I'd fill a bucket with about thirty pounds of raw ground meat and a small bucket of spices that Trofim prepared on his own. ("Top secret," he would say in his thick accent, waving his hands around as if warding off devils.)

Then I would plunge my arms in and mix it manually, working the spices into the cold, gelatinous flesh, taking care to go from top to bottom to top to bottom to top, just as Trofim had shown me. The frigid meat would numb my arms and hands. The odor was foul, the spices accentuating the strange smell of raw meat. I would go to the sink and run my arms under liters of warm water, lathering repeatedly and with futility. The smell was always with me, lingering like a bad memory even after I showered back home.

After the mixing was done, I would pour some of the contents of the bucket into a massive piping bag and run the spiced raw meat in five or six-inch-wide strips down the entire length of the table, each separated by several inches of flattened pastry dough. Once the long rivers of meat were laid down, one of us would run a pizza cutter next to each one and we would hand roll the sausage rolls into four or five fifteen-foot long tubes, which we then sliced using a measured see-sawing tool that could cut all the rows at once. We would put the rolls into one of our deep freezers where they sat on wax-paper-covered trays at minus forty for months.

The freezers were more frightening than the roller. The rule at T&H was that nobody worked alone in the shop, and in particular, *never* went into the freezer unless someone else was there. An hour was enough to kill you at that temperature.

Trofim was a gruff and distant presence. He seemed preoccupied all the time. This was in the late eighties, remember, when General Jaruzelski had imposed martial law in Poland.

One September morning, after I had found my legs, Dylan took me aside. "Give the old man some room today," he said as we put our aprons on. "His sister got arrested yesterday."

"Oh?"

"Yeah. She's in that movement—Solidarity. She's an electrician and her shop refused to work and they came and arrested them all. She's a steward, one of the leaders. He's worried. That's what he told me."

We could hear Trofim walking up the steps.

"I told him he should take the day off. He wouldn't. Just so you know."

Trofim made no sign that day of being nervous, other than being a bit more quiet than usual.

As Dylan and I removed our blood and spice-encrusted frocks and threw them in the big hamper next to the back entrance before leaving for the day, I asked him, "Any news?'

"Not that I know of," Dylan answered. He looked at Trofim as the older man began to disassemble the rolling machine for its daily cleaning, which he always insisted on doing himself.

"He looks like he's dealing with it pretty well."

Dylan raised an eyebrow.

"Don't we all look like that, most of the time?" he said.

#

The next morning, I was a little early grabbing the 26 Crosstown from the two-bedroom basement I shared with Douglas, an Australian student at UVic who seemed to be majoring in weed consumption instead of organic chemistry. I got to the doors of the shop half an hour before the start of my shift. It was a cool but sunny morning, typical of Victoria in late summer, and I sat on the front steps to roll a smoke and enjoy the crisp air when the door opened behind me. I turned to see Trofim, still wearing his jacket.

"Oh, hello Simon," he said. As usual, his accent lent his words a formality he probably didn't intend. He looked at my cigarette. "It smells good," he said.

"Oh—did you used to smoke?"

He smiled. "Oh yes. Far too much, at least according to my wife. She nagged me and nagged me until I stopped." He smelled a tendril of blue smoke that crept up the cool morning air like a thief. "Delicious," he said, his eyes half-closed.

"When did you quit?" I asked, expecting the answer to be six months or a year before.

"Oh God—twenty years ago. I was in the third year at the Krakow University of Technology in Engineering. It was before my exams. I thought maybe I would die." He came back a little. "So as good as that smells, I will never smoke again. I know this, so I allow myself to smell it sometimes." He paused. "You are here early today."

"I left early. We were out of coffee and I stopped at the 7-11 on the way and got an earlier bus."

Trofim pulled up his sleeve to look at his plain, black-banded wristwatch.

"Well I am expecting a delivery soon."

"Oh, I can help."

Trofim shook his head. "Not the usual kind. Not flour or meat. Something different. I would not want your help for this."

He seemed jittery. I realized that his earlier babbling about smoking was the most he had ever said to me in the three months I had been working there. He was nervous.

I heard the truck before I saw it, and once I saw it I knew it was coming to T&H Frozen Foods.

It was a modified F-150 with a rack system for lighting, roll bars, and a tarp in the bed.

And poking out from under the tarp: a hoof up to the knee.

Two men got out of the truck. One was older, maybe in his early forties, wearing a trucker's cap and filthy denim. The other was young and thin, with a wispy suggestion of a beard and deep-set eyes. His already-thinning hair was greasy and stringy looking.

Father and son, I thought.

"Trofim?" the older man said as he shut the truck's door behind him.

Trofim walked toward the truck. He extended his hand and they shook. The tarp-covered thing in the truck continued to extend its hoof into oblivion.

"Name's Todd, but I guess you know that already."

"Yes, Paul told me."

Dylan had told me about Paul Chelkowski. He was Trofim's drinking buddy from the Tudor House. Paul liked to hunt. Now it made sense.

They were here for the freezer.

The young man was already pulling the tarp away, revealing a deer in three bloody acts: right flank, left flank, and head. The organs had been cut out and were no doubt in a steaming and bloody patch of the woods. The eyes were milky with death.

I had never hunted, but I knew this much from talking to my uncle Pete who had kept us in venison when I was a kid: we were weeks out of deer season for the South Island.

The deer was illegally hunted.

I looked at the lights. Maybe they had found the doe on one of the old logging roads in Sooke. They had used the lights to blind her. She had stood there, helpless, and waited for them to kill her.

"Simon," he said. "Could you open the door to the third freezer?"

I nodded and went inside. The two meat bags were in their usual spot next to the table. I walked to the freezer and opened it. A rush of ice vapor enveloped me as I latched it open. There was nothing on the racks and a space had been cleared in the corner.

Trofim had already been at work this morning, making space.

I stood by the roller as the two men carried the first piece in between them. Each of them had a leg. Blood splattered on the white floor. Trofim hovered behind them nervously. The older man huffed and puffed like a giant in a fairy tale.

"How cold you say this was?" the younger one asked as they emerged from the freezer.

"Minus forty," Trofim answered.

"Pretty fucking cold," the young man replied.

"Yes," Trofim said quietly; he didn't like swearing. "Pretty cold."

Ten minutes later, the pieces of deer were in the freezer and the door shut. Trofim went out to the parking lot. I saw the older one open a creased and ancient wallet and pull out several bills, then pass them to Trofim.

As the truck pulled away, I saw the blinds of the Daybreak Tofu shift slightly. There was the barest hint of a twitching finger. Then I heard the truck's brakes squeal as it stopped quickly. Dylan's car then nosed into the little lot, gingerly passing the pickup which sped off as soon as his car had cleared it.

Trofim walked right to Dylan's car as soon as it was parked. Dylan got out, putting his bag on the Skylark's roof. He had a smoke burning in his mouth, and his lips were thin. He hooked a thumb toward Esquimalt Road, and said something. Trofim answered and it looked like Dylan didn't like what he was hearing. He closed his door—a little too hard—and then walked by me without a word.

#

Trofim mopped up the blood. I offered to do it, but he insisted.

Dylan and I smoked outside, waiting for him to finish.

"He's going to catch shit one of these days," Dylan said darkly, his thin nose pointing at the door like an accusation.

"Has he done this before?"

"Yeah. Last year. Twice. Different guys each time, but the same story. Early morning deliveries. His buddy Paul sets it up for him."

"And what—they just leave the carcass in the freezer?"

"No, they'll come and take pieces out soon enough. As soon as they find friends with deep-freezers big enough to help them."

"I wonder what they pay him?" I said.

Dylan took a final drag. "Not enough," he said. "If he gets caught, he could lose his fucking business license."

I finished my smoke. As I tossed it, still burning, into the lot, the front door of Daybreak Tofu opened. An elderly man, his back stooped, stepped out. The proprietor. He'd set up shop in the early seventies. He wore an apron. His long thinning hair was tied back under a hairnet. He nodded at me gravely, pulling out a smoke of his own. His glasses reflected the light and obscured his eyes.

I gave a half-wave, turned, and went back inside to mix the meat.

#

The next morning, there was a heavy knock at the front door. Trofim opened it.

A bearded and serious-looking young man wearing a blue suit stood there and said a few quiet words to Trofim, who nodded and led him into his office in the back.

"You two take an early lunch today," he said. "Come back at one."

"That's in two hours," Dylan responded.

"Yes. Enjoy," Trofim said, closing the door of his office behind him.

#

Having twice our usual time, Dylan and I decided to go to Tommy Tucker's—now long gone—on Admirals Road for a proper sit-down meal. A burger and fries for me and a Salisbury steak for Dylan. We didn't say much during the meal.

As we were leaving, Dylan said, "Trofim's sister is going on trial. It doesn't look good. He told me this morning."

"Is that what that man was doing at the shop?" I asked.

"Maybe," he said. "I know there's a big Polish community in Vancouver who he talks to. Some of them are activists and lawyers. Maybe he came over from there."

#

When we got back, the front door was wide open and Trofim was sitting on the loading ramp, his legs dangling over the asphalt.

"Hello boys," he said.

We got back to work, Trofim joining us for the rest of the shift, though he was even quieter than usual. I saw him look over at the freezer once or twice.

#

The next morning I got there ten minutes before starting time, and was surprised to find the door locked. I pounded a few times without much hope—Trofim's car was nowhere to be seen. I sat and smoked.

A few minutes later, Dylan's Skylark pulled in.

"Where's the old man?" he asked.

I shrugged. "No idea." I paused. "His sister?"

"Yeah. He didn't call me though. He always calls if he can't make it."

Dylan reached into his pocket and pulled out a gaggle of keys held together by a latching ring of the same kind of chrome alloy they make bikes out of. "We can get started without him. I'll call him when we get inside."

He called as I mixed the meat. The door was open. A seagull hobbled back and forth idiotically. It picked up a butt and then dropped it. It screamed and then flew off.

I walked to the sink to rinse and warm my hands as usual. Dylan came out of the office.

"He's on his way," he said.

"Everything alright?"

He shrugged. "Says he overslept. That's bullshit. But he's coming in." His gaze shifted to the freezer.

"When will they come back, do you think?" I said. "Those hunters?"

"Better be fucking soon. The last thing Trofim needs is to lose his license."

We rolled the dough until Trofim showed up half an hour later.

#

He called us in before we drove to Esquimalt Plaza for lunch.

"Try," he said.

The room smelled of baked pastry and savory spices. The little toaster oven Trofim kept in his office had been at work.

Dylan and I each took one-half of the roll on the plate.

"What is this?" Dylan asked suspiciously.

"It is a veggie roll. More and more vegetarians." It was clear that the word was uncomfortable in his mouth. "I made the mix last night. Same spices as the pork and beef. Try!"

I shrugged and took a bite.

"It's good," I said. "Is it tofu?"

"Some, yes," Trofim replied, nodding. "Also chickpeas, oats, and celery, other things."

"Texture's weird," Dylan chimed in. "But the taste is nearly there."

Trofim frowned. "It is hard without fat from the meat. I used some olive and canola oil for mouthfeel, but you are right Dylan. It is not the same."

"Still good," I said. "Good enough for a *vegetarian*, anyway."

We all had a good laugh at that.

#

We had just racked up our last table full of sausage rolls—all-beef this time—and were cleaning the machine when the knock came.

It sounded official. No-nonsense. Unfeeling. Four raps that rang like the snare of an 808. Dylan moved toward the door but Trofim emerged from his office.

"Wait, wait," he said. "Let me." He turned to us. "You boys go home."

But we stood there as he opened the door. A middle-aged woman with a clipboard stood there, a younger and chubbier man behind her. Both of them had identity cards on dongles around their necks. Business casual clothes.

"I'm Jennifer Dileep," she said. "From the Canadian Food Inspection Agency. This is Jonathan Wile."

"How do you do," said the fatter man.

"Are you Trofim Gryzbowski, proprietor of T&H Frozen Foods?" she asked, reading from her clipboard and mangling his name. All business.

"Yes."

"We have had a report that there may be contaminants on-site. May we come in?" she said.

"Do I have a choice?" Trofim asked.

"No. We are authorized to enter the premises," she replied. "This is a spot inspection. You have to let us in."

"Very well," said Trofim with a sigh. "I assume you have paperwork?"

"Of course."

She filed through the contents of the clipboard and pulled out several pieces of paper. She peeled two off and handed them to Trofim.

"These are yours to keep, Mr. Gryzbowski."

Trofim squinted at the text and nodded.

"Who made the report?" he asked.

"Can't tell you that," said the man. He had the smallest hint of a grin. He liked his job.

"Well, come in," Trofim said.

"We want to see the freezers," the woman said. She looked around the shop. Dylan and I remained next to the roller as the three of them walked by.

Trofim opened the first of the walk-in freezers. I heard the woman ask him some questions, but the words were obscured.

They got to the last of the walk-ins, where the deer was. Trofim hesitated the slightest bit, his hand hovering over the latch like an anxious mother.

Trofim opened the door and the three of them went inside. I bit my lower lip until it started to bleed.

They emerged a few seconds later. The woman pointed to the office door and Trofim opened it. They went inside.

"Smoke?" I said.

"Yeah."

Dylan and I went to the parking lot and stood next to the black sedan that had brought the food inspectors. We lit up, not saying anything.

A few minutes later, they emerged from the front door, Trofim behind them. They looked disappointed as they walked by us and got into the car. The doors shut softly; it was a nice car.

Dylan and I smoked. I watched the two in the car. The woman had the clipboard open and a pen in her hand. She wrote as the two of them talked, the man at the wheel.

After a couple of minutes, the car pulled out of the parking lot and onto Esquimalt Road, its tires crunching bits of gravel and crumbling asphalt.

Trofim came and stood with us.

"My sister smokes," he said. "Nasty habit."

"It is," Dylan agreed. He reached into his pocket and pulled out a pack of Sportsman's. He held it out to our boss, who nodded and took one out. I passed him my Zippo and Trofim cupped his hands like a sailor as he lit up. He coughed to the point of retching at first—it had been a long time, clearly—but then settled into the old poison by the third drag.

We watched the traffic on Esquimalt Road. Cars going opposite directions at equal speed. Same as usual.

"Three years," Trofim said. "'*Crimes against the peace of the state.*'" He spat onto the parking lot, but didn't cough or say another word. Dylan patted the older man on the shoulder.

We finished our cigarettes and said goodnight.

Preparedness
Alex Wells Shapiro

～

Between streetlights in a sunken gated
alley accordion playing bare arms extending

and collapsing their instrument
accompanying a distorted boom-
box mosquito lamp sizzling above

their ear my sharp lateral stagger around a
hydrant cap tilt obscuring acknowledgment
melody continuing co-mingling in sirens

horns yelps flecked constellations furnishing
the outskirts of our block (occupied by
tunneled wind shepherding leaves

and litter toward lakefront and their song)
raised skin ebbing supple shrunk to non-
confrontational normalcy as I perceive no

                                      other in front of me.

                              Clear **intersection** outlined
                              white thru solid rain-lurching
                              into a trot across tracking
                              Skid Honk Crunsh behind me.

Transfusion
A. A. deFreese

~

When she slipped me the Jehovah's Witness card on the last day of classes, on the low key across the front desk after we had already said our goodbyes, I opened my purse and handed her my mother's kidney donor card. It was automatic. It seemed a fair exchange. I might have given her my soul, in disbelief, had she matched.

We both thanked each other without looking up from our cards. At first glance, I thought I had won something, that *JW* was some hotel, one of those appreciation vouchers we raffled at the annual breakfast, good for a stay at a 24-hour paradise with room service, a kidney-shaped pool chlorinated to tears, but no traces of red on the water.

I should have known about the transfusions, though. The weeks following the "event," we had screened PG *Selena*—and the documentary about making it—on the flat screen repeatedly in all my Spanish classes because no one could focus.

Had she been spreading the good news to students, too, when they stopped for a mini Snickers from the jarful of offerings attached to no particular season? Sliding in these cards when she passed a tampon to the ones caught early who always left late because there was no particular place to call home beyond the front office sofa? As she handed out morning pencils to the ones who cut at lunch?

Looking up again, we said nothing about our card exchange, and both hoped we would see each other in September. But I knew I couldn't teach there next fall after the blood in the cafeteria. A door snapping shut suddenly was enough to make me jump, the wind at the window, a falling thesaurus, the rattle of glass when they wheeled out the recycling after filling the machines. It hadn't made national news. After all, only four were wounded—not twenty—but the helicopters had tapped overhead anyway.

One dropped out to have her baby, two transferred; another, still on crutches, would never play basketball again.

Over the summer break, I always forgot. Maybe I would be back. It had been a pretty normal school year, actually. Mom was improving, her nephrologists said, there had been no new fires in the Gorge since late 2017, and no one had overdosed or been stabbed in the bathroom last year.

And anyway, who knew? Wasn't 2019-2020 bound to be better?

Aphorism 30
John Blair

~

The clawed beasts of worry watch and wait
    neither blood nor snow   but a fog
of in-between with misty teeth frozen
into spindles   to gnaw my nervy edges
into wakefulness   until I start to long
for loud   for a shout from the brink
    where the bad boys and girls loiter
caffeine hot   & scratching dogmas
on the walls with a sound magma-ish
as the mutter of continents sliding like cars
on black ice   like razors shaving reason
into ever thinner shades of coherence
    until anger alone is almost enough.

*digital art by
Angie Cruz*

from
Siena Diaries
Angie Cruz
2021 Gina Berriault Award recipient
~

I was lost on the winding streets of Siena. It was around 3 p.m. and most people were napping or evading the heat. Just me on the streets. A man poked his head out from a window and asked in Italian, What are you doing right now? I said, I don't know? Honestly, I really didn't know. I had been writing all morning and needed to take a walk. Then he said, Wait there, okay? So I waited and thought maybe like it happens in the movies this beautiful Italian man would spontaneously take me on a long walk, buy me a gelato and show me his favorite buildings. I waited and waited because the entrance to the building was on the other side of the street. But suddenly I heard the piano, the music coming from his window. The streets were deserted. It was 93 degrees that day. I sat on some steps of the building opposite the window. I closed my eyes and listened.

I took this photo and then I read the sign: It is prohibited to take photos or video. The sign was posted at the pig's request. Of course, I apologized and then the pig told me that she did not ask to be hung there, disembodied, a spectacle to be gawked at. It's bad enough she was cut in parts, sliced, and cured. That for many months, maybe even years, she's had no choice but to hang there and watch people ogle and devour her parts. So I told her that in protest I will not eat any pork. Then she said, You mean after all my sacrifice, you won't even give me the dignity to be eaten? So I told her I will discard this photo. I will at least do as her sign requests. But she said, first let me look at it. I borrowed a pair of glasses from a tourist eating a gelato, placed it on the pig's snout so she could see better. She was quite pleased with the photo and said, Che Bella porchetta! Save it.

When I got on the train from Siena to Florence I was alone, relieved that I was finally sitting and could read my book. This woman sat across from me. She said good morning, pulled out rolling paper, her pouch of tobacco and rolled a cigarette. I assumed it was for later. There were signs everywhere that we were in the nonsmoking car. But she lit it. Inhaled, exhaled, and looked right at me then out the window. She's breaking the rules, I wanted to tell someone with authority. But we were alone. Why sit across from me when the car was empty? She could've gone to the other end of the car. But it was as if she needed me to witness her smoking unapologetically, to fully enjoy that cigarette. A smile escaped her lips. I was tempted to cough, to seemed bothered by the smoke but her disregard for the rules, even for my judgement was overwhelmingly sexy. Isn't this what we want from our stories, for our characters to surprise us, to do what we are not capable of doing?

SPECIAL FEATURE

~

This year's theme: black-and-white artwork, created within the margins of neurodivergence. *Fourteen Hills* received an array of submissions, and we are pleased to present the pieces that awed, surprised, and excited us most.

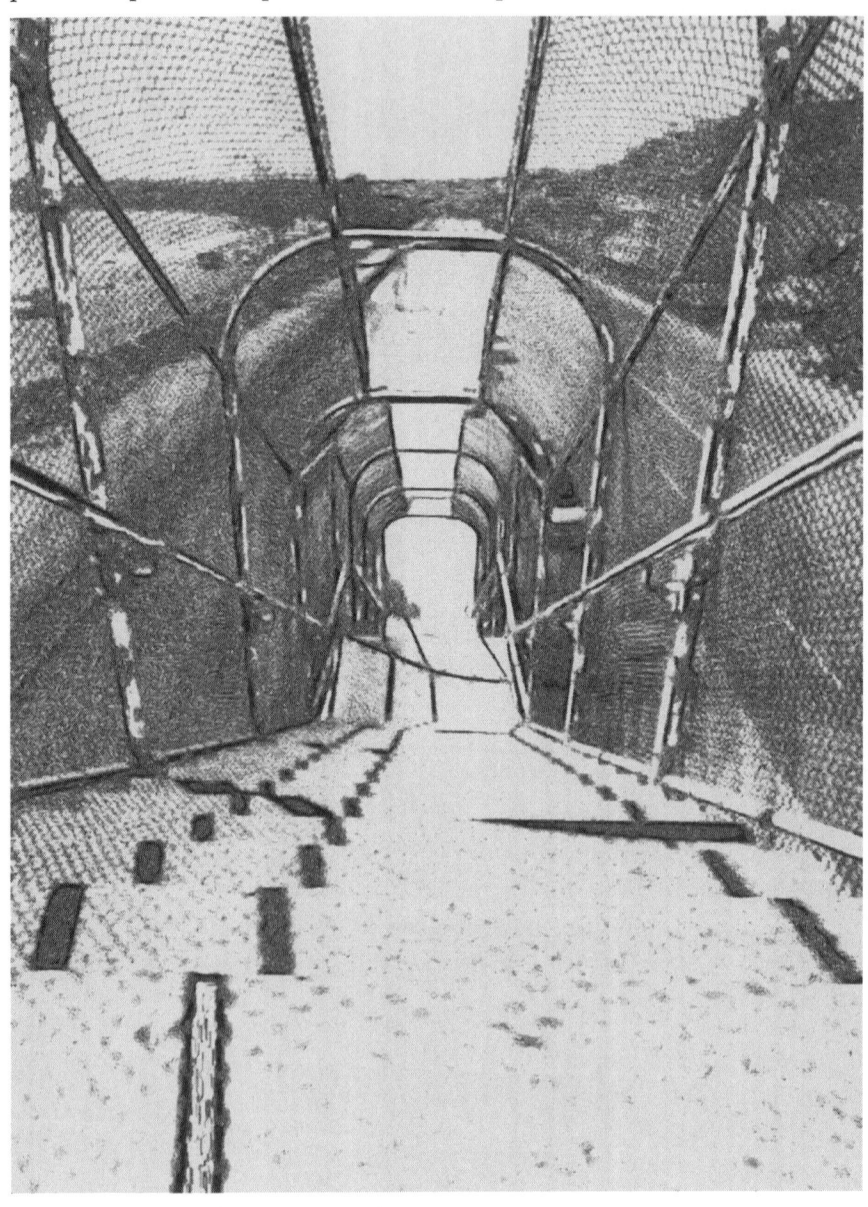

STAIRS

three digital photographs
Christopher Strople

TRESTLES *(above)* & **POND**

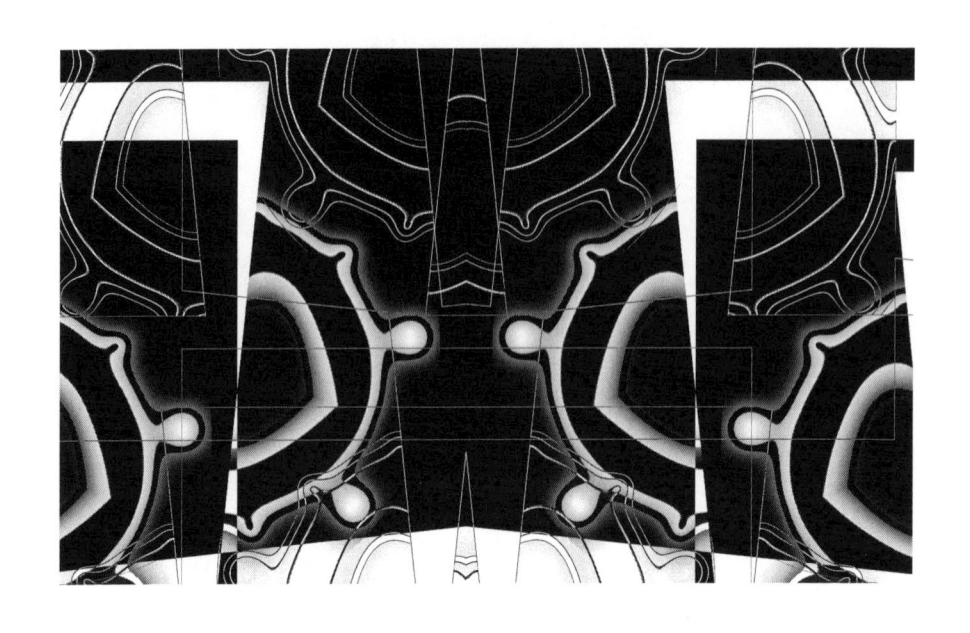

Darkness Looms #3
&
Darkness Looms #4
Edward Michael Supranowicz

digital paintings made with GIMP

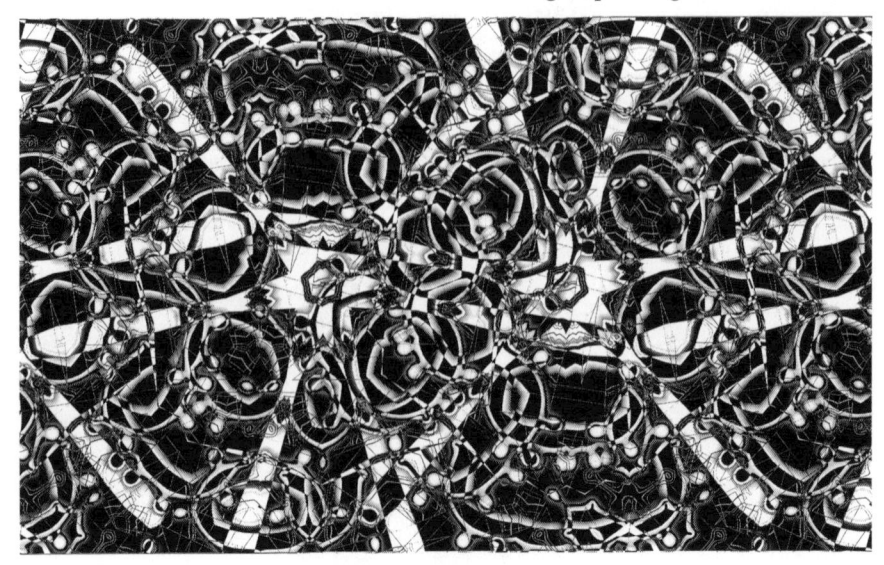

What Lies Beneath
Grace Wagner

pen-and-ink
5" × 5"

Rococo Dreams
Grace Wagner

pen-and-ink
8.5" × 10"

Damn Spot
Grace Wagner

pen-and-ink
8.5" × 11"

Resurrection
Natasha Huey

~

let me come back as something without a footprint   like a moth or thunder

let me come back as something that hurts nothing   i hope there is such a thing

let me come back as something barely perceptible   but monumental

    four leaf clover in a field

       oxygen in the rubble

          pinprick of ink in a first tattoo

let me return useful

    aloe

       honey bee

          kidney perhaps

let me reawaken humble

    graphite the plainest jewel

       single stalk of wheat

          praying mantis eaten by a lover

                              or none at all

                                              but gentler

let me come back as something less poison

let me come back as something with more foresight

let me come back

        and try this wild world again

Who Is an Individual
Natasha Huey

∽

with a skeleton of so many bones? a power grid of nerves strung under the skin. enough muscles to swing an axe and lift an eyelid. enough hair follicles to outnumber the population of Los Angeles. enough dna unspooled to lasso the solar system. a brain full of inherited language dependent on another brain to learn their own function, location, name. an individual? what does that make the alveoli or vertebrae? the bustling streets of blood delivering packages of oxygen and vitamins and squeezing past crowds of soldiers and salts. when whole professions are dedicated to learning the names of everyone inside you? there's not a person on the planet whose atoms you haven't inhaled. come on. independent? from what? from whom? singular like a library? a book? a word? a letter? every solo you know is already an ensemble. the collective: a body you're born into.

A Name
Natasha Huey

~

Natasha:
                that is Russian name

the young uber driver says to me
leaning back in his leather seat
looking for home in my face
what city is your family from?
do you speak Russian?

the tow truck driver from the army
the bartender in the tight, dark venue
the second, third, fourth lyft driver
               to ask
               Russia?
               Ukraine?
               Romania?
               do you speak Romanian?
               what city are you from?
the man in the Vegas club who grabs my hand to his lips whispering in Russian
      with a hunger every woman can translate

I search for what must be familiar to these men
what to me is just a blur of my uncle, brother, mom
and blends with every other white girl face on the train

               I don't know the name
               of the village
               in what is now Ukraine

                   I only know

                        it was extracted
                        from the map
                        like a fingernail
ripped
at the root
                    in WWII

                I imagine burst buildings
like blown dandelions
roads naked of traffic
plumbing visible as exposed bone

I only know
that Rebecca Soibelman
and her five children
had faces
the Germans recognized
a name
less dangerous
to carry to Ellis Island
than at home

I only know
that no one spoke
Russian to the children

Know Yourself
Valeria Amirkhanyan

mixed media on canvas
70 cm × 90 cm

Moth Mountain
Kate Gardiner

pen-and-ink
11" × 14"

Etto, 1959
Cameron Moreno

~

I'd heard about Etto before, but only in passing. Once, in the middle of one of Grandpa's war stories, he said Etto's name, then his face turned solid. I pressed on, asked him who Etto was, where he was now. Grandpa said it was simple: Etto was there, then he wasn't.

That was a few years ago.

Now, Grandpa was settled in the main bedroom of the house while he recovered from open-heart surgery. He spent most of his time resting, always tired from trying to survive. I spent that time cleaning around the house: the kitchen, then the backyard, then the spare room. While reorganizing the spare room, re-boxing the guts of memories to last another however-many-years in new cardboard homes, I found a stack of photos tied together with a rubber band. Some were of him and Grandma, young with perfectly coifed hair and vintage clothes. Some were of my aunts and uncles as children, playing in the yard, posed on the first day of school, reaching for the camera with their cherubic face brilliant from the flash. Then, one in black and gray of a handsome man. Flexed arms, shirtless, his back to whomever took the picture. His muscles reminded me of waves glistening in the sun. His veins a lightning storm. On the back of the photo, scribbled in cursive: *Etto, 1959*.

Grandpa woke from his nap, and we ate chicken soup. When he'd fished and caught the last noodle out of the clouded soup, I placed Etto's photo on the empty space of mattress between us.

For a moment he stared at it as though it would tell him something. He smiled.

"Oh," he said. It was quiet, what you say when your heart is tender, when it opens up and your body fills with a welcoming warmth. He showed it to me. "You know who took this?"

I shook my head.

"I did. He was beautiful."

Grandpa told me the photo was from when the two of them were twenty-something. I could see them, young, not yet drafted, not yet married, spending all summer building boats for a local surf shop, something Grandpa insisted he could still do if he had the dexterity. Somewhere in the afternoon of stories, Grandpa confessed he'd seen Etto in the sleep of surgery. It wasn't a dream so much as it was a memory: the two were on Bob Hall Pier eating gelato. Etto had been drafted and was leaving that next week. Grandpa would follow three weeks later, but they didn't know that yet. As the two of them watched the waves crash on the shore, Etto told Grandpa he loved him. It was the first time Grandpa heard this from another man—he had no brothers and his father was absent as air.

    I listened, waited to hear if Grandpa had said it back to him.

Hiraeth
Catherine Kyle

A Welsh word, hiraeth refers to a feeling characterized by longing, nostalgia, and remorse.

My slate turtleneck has shrunk in the wash.
Now, when I walk, the hem brushes the navel
piercing I once fetched as a lure. In the cramped
dark shop that overlooked the sea. Turning out
girls with jewels in their guts. Sparkling like
anglerfish.

The birch trees lean over a chain link fence
that claims to delineate footpath from shore.
But see here, it ends. Inviting the truth. Inviting
trespass in this river. Take my hand—it is
muddy, this part of the slope. I don't want you
falling in.

In the recurring dream I had as a child that taught
me the meaning of hunger, a man shows up
on the doorstep of a woman who had thought
he was dead. Her heart is stampeding, but she acts
casual. She chatters and heats up the kettle for tea
until she is harpooned with a kiss.

I lied. It wasn't a dream, but a wish, something seen
penciled in storm clouds. The birch trees are peeling
their bark from themselves. And I am an orange
with the rind pulled back—a pulpy orb of a heart.
The gemstone that punctures me glitters through
fabric. A lighthouse. A siren. A song.

Glitter Camo Girl
Catherine Kyle

~

in the metro is a girl with a glitter camo backpack.

a camouflage designed to catch the light.   so pretty.   imagine—

a sequined celebration.

                              imagine   needing   camouflage like that—

where

would you be hiding?   and hiding

from what?

the article mentions   acres of bodies.   charred,

*

now.   acres of bodies.   we tell

some animals   might become myths,   things   protection from something

our children about.

imagine   needing

as normal as fire,   continent-wide.

*

a student in the metro   says to his friend: *last summer,*   *I built*

a machine gun.

imagine   other nouns   that noun could be: *last summer,*   *I built*

a pillow fort. a tree house.   *last summer, I built*   *better friendships.*   *last summer,*

I built   a basketful of canned food.   *I left it on my brother's   front porch.*

a girl in the metro in a glitter camo backpack.   *disguised.*

disguised   as what?

*

is there a name for this feeling?

GLITTER CAMO GIRL   81

not personal grief— but species grief, a global grief,

expanding.

the turnip of my heart turns a little. rotates wetly.

everywhere, the odor of ash.

*

the headline hovers over a photograph of polar bears, ribs protruding,

seated on a throne of old Coke cans.

I do not click the headline. I do not click the headline. but I think I catch the words

extinction grief.

*

all things end.

some say, *this isn't unusual. unspecial— unspecial unspecial*

we are, in our grief.

a girl in a glitter camo backpack is holding her tall father's hand. a child. a schoolgirl.

she looks young to be wearing   combat chic, but   unsure how to live in a body.
sometimes I want to disappear, too.

*

who was camouflaging   their babies against   the roar of the fire?
disintegrating trees?
who will camouflage me   against the spin of bullets   emitting from a summer gun
like silver?   like light?

*

scrolling   and scrolling   through three different apps,   I'm looking—
I'm looking—
for answers.
so many experts. discourse, so quick.   surely,
they must be here somewhere.
I click *like* on babies   and warm bread   and glitter   and lipstick   and new cars
and gravy.

I click *like.*   I click *like.*   my red heart flies

through channels   all monitored by men.

imagine   it bouncing   off satellites' skins—   my heart in space,

then landing in pixels.

*

the planet turns red.   a red heart   in space.   a fire. immaculate   fire.

last summer, I picked off   my sequins   like scales—

and what did I find there?   just raw, aching flesh.   just vulnerable,

   raw, aching flesh.   imagine—   if I touch it   to a burner,

what then?   a searing.   an ecocide of cells.

*

a girl in the metro has a glitter camo backpack.

so flashy. so militaristic.   what kind of landscape   could she be in?

   what kind of land   could demand this?

Eddie's Mom
Ciaran Cooper

CONTENT WARNING: *contains offensive language.*

I already told you some about Eddie's mom, how she's got gray hair in a long braid down her back and a broken tooth and how her veins pop out all blue on her arms and how her eyes get mean when she plucks a chicken, how the bones in her wrist stick out and her ears too, and how Eddie looks just like her, broken tooth and all, 'cept he walks like his dad and his hair's greasy brown not gray.

And I already told you how she hits Eddie with a belt for stuff he didn't always do and how she made my mother cry at my brother's funeral. How one time she taught me to kill a chicken the right way, one quick chop with a hatchet then you tie bailing twine around its feet and hang it on the shed door so it won't run off getting blood all over the place with the dogs chasing it around the yard all day.

That was three years ago, before I could work the pump handle outside the barn, before Colin died and I got my own room and we stopped going to church.

But I never told you everything.

Like how Eddie's mom used to make Eyes of God out of yarn and sticks, and hanging plant baskets with soft rope and wooden beads that she sold at church or the farm stand on Miller's Road. And how after Colin died she was always saying I should buy one for my mother for her birthday or Christmas or Mother's Day. You owe your life to your mother, why don't you do something nice for her, she'd say, so one day I gave her five dollars I saved up in dimes and nickels and she let me pick one of each. I chose a hanging basket made with yellow beads and an Eye of God with purples and blues. She said, I should charge you double that one's so nice, but I said that was all the money I had and she said, Don't worry I'm just joshin' ya, go on take it home to your mother.

So I put them both in a brown paper bag and colored *I love you Mom* on it and stuffed in some leftover purple Easter grass to make it a surprise, but when my mother saw the Eye of God, she didn't smile like I thought she would, she just said, What the hell does that woman know about God? Then she told me I should take it back because we didn't need anything from her ever, so Eddie and me hung the Eye of God on a tree trunk and used it for target practice. The basket we hung in the back of their shed where Eddie's mom never goes and some birds made a nest in it. We watched the baby chicks hatch like little dinosaurs while we ate candy bars his sister Cheryl stole from Peoples Drug.

But I want to tell how last week I rode up to Eddie's house just hanging around riding circles in the dirt seeing if maybe he could come outside so I yelled up and he was running through the kitchen when his mom caught him at the screen door yelling, Go git them eggs like I told you Gotdamnit! and she swiped at his head but he ducked out onto the porch and down the stairs in one giant moon jump. Then Eddie's mom came out on the porch and said, You there! pointing at me riding circles in the dirt still, so I kick-stopped my bike and shuffled up to the porch and she handed me a wicker basket as high as my knees. She said since I was there I could help Eddie get the eggs and clean out the coop before we run off doin' no good all day. Eddie stood in the daylilies watching me sweat, taking the basket, and saying Yes ma'am as polite as I could say it, and when his mom turned away he threw a dirtball that hit me in the arm and ran toward the coop so I knew the war was on when I came through the door.

I used the basket as a shield when he threw a pile of chicken shit and straw at me and it fell on my new Pumas I bought at the secondhand store in town. I swung the basket and hit him in the head then ran to where they keep the fresh straw. We were stuffing it down each other's shirts and swinging it like whips at each other's faces laughing, but then Eddie picked up an egg. He threw it and missed by a mile. It exploded against the wire cages and the chickens started squawking like crazy birds.

We called truce right away because we knew if we both started throwing eggs Eddie'd get a beating for sure and we'd prolly never see each other ever again. I said, We should get the eggs before anything bad happens. Eddie held the basket while I gathered them, careful not to lay them down too hard, some of them still warm where the hens were roosting on them a minute ago and some of them covered in feathers and chicken shit like glue. We packed straw in the bottom of the basket to stop them rolling all over the place and cracking before we got them back to the house. After a while the smell in there was killing us and we were barely halfway done. We had to keep opening the door to let the breeze in but there wasn't much wind blowing and the day was getting hotter, the sun already over the trees coming down straight on us.

After we got all the eggs in the basket, I asked Eddie should I go get the pitchforks but Eddie was leaning over with his asthma real bad and he said, Fuck this, let's get of here, go to the swimming hole or something, I'm gonna be sick if we spend one more fucking minute in here, and I was glad he said it because I wanted to get out of there too. Eddie cusses a lot but not as much as his mother. It's cuz now he's in eighth grade he hangs out with his sister and her high school friends and they cuss all the time. His favorite new word is fuck. Sometimes he just walks along going fuck fuck fuck. My new favorite is shitpecker, but I don't get to say it as much as Eddie gets to say fuck. He says fuck this, fuck that, fuck you, fuck that fuck, fuck fuck fuck, fucking fuck, but every now and then I say, Man what a shitpecker, and that cracks us up so it's not so bad saving it I guess.

Eddie's mom needed the eggs for the farm stand and she was already late getting her muffins out the oven and they burned, so she was in a bad mood already. Plus she was mad the crows got to the tomatoes so she didn't have hardly any to take, but we knew if we were quick and quiet we could sneak away instead of helping her all day at the roadside stand that hardly anyone ever stops at. Eddie put the basket on the porch while I stood at the bottom of the stairs. He poked his head inside yelled, Ma! The eggs! then to me, Come on! and we were running superfast across the yard toward the woods when Eddie's mom yelled out the window, Gotdamnit! I told you to clean that coop! but we couldn't hear the rest we were laughing so loud and running until Eddie couldn't get his breath and we had to stop but by then we were already gone.

Eddie's got lots of chores to do like cleaning out the bird coops or watering the cows or bagging corn or picking beans or whatever his mother tells him to do after breakfast, but I don't have too many so I usually help him with his. We don't have a cow anymore since we ate Olga. We just have Gracie now, our pony, plus our horse Flicker and only a few chickens not a whole coop-full, and no ducks or geese either like at Eddie's farm.

Last summer my dad ran a water line from the shed to the paddock so all I have to do now is turn it on and wait for the bathtub to fill and maybe wipe away some of the slime that floats in there. That and throw Flicker and Gracie fresh hay. Twice a week I muck out the stalls but that's about all because my mother grows our vegetables herself and we get milk and eggs from the other farms. We also have our dog Crusoe, but he's chained to a tree out front now because last summer he chased a girl who used to live on the farm at the bottom of the road and he bit most of her ear off. We didn't get in trouble, though, and they didn't have to shoot Crusoe because the girl shouldn't have been running across our yard, plus my parents paid the hospital bills. She got about ninety stitches in her ear and then they moved away.

Oh yeah, and we have rabbits too but they just eat carrot peels and potato skins my mom saves in a brown paper shopping bag. Sometimes I dump the whole bag in there and sometimes I feed them one piece at a time just to feel them pull it from my hand. So my work is done pretty fast, maybe an hour after breakfast, and if I ride to Eddie's right away we can get everything done at his house before lunchtime.

On the way to the tree fort we passed Eddie's dad driving the tractor with Mr. Mills and Obie on the back holding chain saws so we hid in case he wanted us to help him bust wood all day. Once they tractored past, we bellyslid down the hill pretending there were Germans on the other ridge and we had to take their radio tower. Then we made a run for the stream where we argued about were we gonna keep playing German U-boat or switch to *Captain Zemo's Danger Island*, my latest comic. We did rock paper scissors and Eddie won so we played German U-boat where we had to set explosives and then swing across the harbor to safety before they blew.

There's really two treehouses but one's just a platform made of saplings we tied into the tree with baling string, and the other one is our tree fort submarine with walls and an escape hatch and everything. It can fit up to four people. We used old barn boards to build it so it looks more real. We add more to it all the time, grabbing things from Eddie's barn and stuff we find in the fields. Like we found these round windows in the barn that we use for portholes and an old stove pipe for our periscope, but you can't really see out of it.

Plus we've got a tire swing that goes over a dried-up part of the stream that's left over from Hurricane Agnes. You can drop off the tire and land in the soft dirt at the bottom. I used to get scared because you have to climb way up high in the tree and jump on while standing up to make it all the way across, but now I like to go as high as I can and lean way back so the ground runs fast away below me and my feet point straight up into the sky. At the highest part, right before the other side, I like to let go and fall backwards into the soft dirt where the water used to run before the hurricane changed the way the stream flows. Even Eddie's too afraid to do that.

So we were swinging from the dock on one side to the submarine on the other and trying not to fall into the harbor. I only fell twice not counting the one time Eddie pushed me. On my last turn, I was as high as I could go waiting to swing back when Brian Mills and a bunch of high school kids came walking up. Sometimes Eddie hangs out with them because they know his sister but I don't really like when they're around, especially Brian. He's always calling me names and pushing me into cow pies and stuff like that and Eddie laughs because he's too scared not to. I hate when Eddie does that. He's afraid of Brian but he won't admit it. He acts like just because he's starting high school next year they're his friends but they're not. Walking with Brian was also some boy I didn't know plus Willow too, whose mother runs a church camp, and her two friends, Becky and Sarah. When I saw them walk up I lost my grip on the rope and fell into the empty streambed.

 I didn't want to come up at first but I was kind of scared to stay down there cuz we saw a snake earlier that Eddie said was a copperhead, and even though Brian's a shitpecker, I think Willow's nice. Once when I was young and my parents had to take Colin to the city for some tests, they sent me to Willow's mom's camp for a whole week where she let me stay up late with her, making Jesus candles in rubber molds. Her hair smelled like crabapple jelly. She told me I didn't have to go to the prayer meetings if I didn't want to, and I didn't and neither did she, so we drank grape juice and I kept her company in her room where the junior counselors lived.

 So Brian came up to the edge of the pit kicking dirt down on me and said, What you doing down there, little maggot? and everyone laughed, I don't know why. I said, Nuthin', just hanging out, but Brian just ignored me and said, Hey Eddie, where's your sister at? and Eddie said he didn't know and Brian said, Well tell her I'm looking for her and Eddie said, Fucking tell her yourself, but when Brian walked over to Eddie and held his fist up Eddie flinched, which cost him two hits to the shoulder and they looked like they hurt. You wanna keep playing your sissy games or you wanna come with us? Brian said.

 I said, We're not sissies and we're doing our own thing, but then Eddie said he wanted to go with them and since I didn't want to be alone I said I'd go too.

 We walked out of the woods into the back field and followed the power lines all the way past Tucker's Pond, and after about a mile we cut back into the woods again to an old house that had a tree growing out of its roof. All the windows were broken out and there were mattresses on the floors upstairs and some old furniture that was full of mouse nests and smelled like piss. Behind the house there was a built-in swimming pool that also had a tree growing up out of the middle and the back end of an old yellow Ford sticking out of it like it crash-landed from outer space.

After we explored for a while, Brian smoked a Kool on the cracked front steps and gave one to his friend whose name it turned out was Peter. Peter and Brian were both seniors in high school. The girls and Willow were all sophomores and Eddie's sister Cheryl was a junior. She's supposed to be a senior with Brian but she got held back a year. Brian tried to get the girls to smoke but they wouldn't. Then Eddie said he wanted one and Brian laughed when he tried to smoke it and started coughing. Brian asked Eddie again where his sister was, like he didn't believe him the first time or something, and Eddie said he didn't know, prolly in town or something, or maybe at work. Cheryl works part-time at Peoples Drug where we go to steal gum and fruit pies. Brian said, Well tell her I was looking for her, tell her she owes me and I need some more smoke, and he gave Eddie a look I couldn't figure out. When he turned around I asked Eddie what Brian meant since he already had a whole pack of Kools in his shirt and Peter had a pack of Marlboros and Eddie just said, I'll tell you later, but he never did.

Then Brian and Willow went up into the house for a little while and left us all sitting on the steps. I wanted to go in and explore some more because I wanted to build a fort in one of the upstairs bedrooms or maybe break some glass. I wanted Brian and Peter to leave so I could talk to Willow like we did at camp that time, but there was just no way. After a while Brian yelled for Peter and the girls to come inside, But tell those turkeys to stay out there, he said, so Peter told me and Eddie we couldn't go in. I was getting pretty bored waiting for something to happen or for Brian to leave and I didn't know why Eddie wanted to stay. After a while I started throwing rocks into the pool and then Eddie started throwing them too. We were trying to hit the taillights out of the car but we kept missing.

Then Brian and the others finally came out and by then the sun was shining on the water and it went from black to green. Brian took his shirt off and laid down in the sun next to Willow showing off his muscles. Willow took her jean jacket off and she was wearing a light blue tube top underneath with dancing bears on it. The other girls took their jackets off too and Peter lit another cigarette. Pretty soon Eddie went over and sat kind of near them. He took his shirt off too showing his skinny white bird chest and laid down in the sun but I stayed where I was.

I was lying on my stomach watching Willow, trying to figure out why she liked Brian, prolly cuz he's a senior and he's got muscles and an eight-track player in his truck, or maybe it's his smile that fooled her, I don't know, but Brian saw me looking and called me a creep. Willow said, Don't tease him, he's okay, and I wanted to hug her for that. I wanted to bury my face in her soft crabapple hair. I wanted her to tell Brian to go away. I wanted them all to go away, even Eddie cuz I don't like him when he's around them. He acts like he's not even my friend.

Then Brian said, He's just trying to get a look at your boobs, and I said, Fuck you, Brian, but when he stood up and said, What'd you say? I wimped out and just said, Nuthin' but I knew he was right. I couldn't help looking. Willow said, Aw leave him alone, Brian, but Brian wouldn't. He sat down again next to Willow and said, Let's go skinny dipping. That way the little shit can see your boobs and we can too, but Willow just pushed him and said, Quit it. No seriously, Brian said, show him your boobs, and after a while I was standing in front of Willow and the other girls and they were lifting their shirts for me and Eddie to see their boobs. I was excited but it also made me kind of dizzy. Then Brian said, Show him your snatch, and she said, Fuck you, Brian, but I wanted to see. Look at him, he wants to see, Brian said, and then Willow asked me if I really did and I nodded my head but I couldn't speak. So Willow said, Come over here then, because I'm not showing it to everyone, and the other girls giggled. Willow took my hand and pulled me toward the other side of the pool. She was wearing pink shorts with white trim. I could see the blonde fuzz on her legs in the sunlight. She told me to stand really close and then she pulled her shorts and her underwear away from her body and I looked down into her pants. She had blonde hair down there too. It looked soft and I wanted to touch it. I could smell baby powder on her stomach. Then she said, Okay that's enough, and she let her shorts snap back against her body.

Now you have to show me yours, she said, but I didn't want to. She said, Hey, fair's fair, so I pulled my shorts away the same way she did and she looked, but Brian was sneak attack behind me and he pulled my shorts down to my sneakers and said, Show her the whole thing you little faggot. I tried to pull them back up but Brian held my hands and lifted me up by my hair. I tried to kick him but he was too strong plus my shorts were around my ankles and I was afraid I might cry when Willow said, Leave him alone he's just a kid, and Brian said, I know he's just a kid, look at that little hairless shrimp between his legs, and everyone laughed, even Willow, and I was trying even harder not to cry. Brian finally let go, but before I could pull my pants up he said, Yeah look at that little thing, man, no girl's ever gonna want to touch that ugly lizard and I started to cry then for real because I wanted Willow to like me. I pulled my pants up and ran back to the other side of the pool and sat by myself.

Willow called Brian a jerk and told him to leave me alone or else she wouldn't let him kiss her again, so he left me alone for a while and pretty soon everyone forgot about it except for me. It was sticky hot out by then so I took my shirt off too finally and laid down near the others. I was wearing my brother's silver medal our mother got him from the gift shop at church once. It's got a picture of Saint Dymphna, some lady who's supposed to watch over kids like Colin, but he died anyway from his seizures. It used to hang from the bedpost above his head. I guess it was supposed to bless him when he slept but after he died I always wore it under my shirt.

After a while Eddie sat down next to me and said, Are you okay?

I was glad he was there but I was mad at him for not doing anything to help me so I ignored him. I just kept twirling the medal between my fingers. The sunlight was bouncing off the silver and making a reflection so I was pretending it was a ray gun and shining it at Brian's head so his fat brain would explode.

Then Eddie rolled over and said, What did it look like?

What? I said.

What do you think, Willow's snatch, he said.

I didn't like that word and I didn't want to tell him what it looked like so I just said, I'll tell you later, but I never did.

It was getting even hotter by then so Brian said Come on, let's go swimming and he stuck his foot into the water, but everyone said no way, there's probably water moccasins in there. Brian said, Chicken shits, and he stripped off his clothes and dove in naked. He swam all the way across and back, splashing water at all of us and calling us pussies. Then he got out and tried to push Peter in but Peter fought him off and lit another cigarette. Sarah grabbed her jacket and said Let's sneak into Tucker's Pond, there's no snakes in there. Brian pulled his jeans back on and said, You guys are all chicken shits but I know someone who wants to go in, and then he grabbed me by the arm and tried to throw me in but I held onto his leg so he'd have to go in with me. Then he ripped my medal off and threw it into the pool and it dropped down into the green-black water and was gone. I jumped up and swung at him but he just knocked me down. I screamed, That was my brother's medal you shitpecker! but the tears were coming so fast I couldn't get the words out right and I ran to the other side of the pool before he could catch me.

Willow said, You're such a dick sometimes Brian, and walked away with Sarah. The others followed and then Peter said, Way to go, turkey, as he walked away with the girls. They all left except for me and Eddie who sat by the edge of the pool looking down through the water for the medal. After they were gone and I stopped crying I told Eddie I had to go get it. He said, What about the snakes? but I didn't care. It took me a long time to build up my nerves but I didn't want to leave without it so I jumped in and swam down with my eyes open in the green water. I couldn't see anything but the water wasn't that deep at that end of the pool, so I ran my hand along the bottom. It was slimy and cold and I was so scared I lost my breath a couple of times and had to come up for air. Eddie had a giant stick to haul me out in case I got stuck on the bottom or the snakes got me. The fourth time I went down I felt the broken chain under my fingers and grabbed it. I got out of the pool and tied the chain in a knot then slipped it back over my head all crooked and messed up. Eddie said, That's the bravest stupid thing you've ever done, and we both laughed. Then he pulled a bunch of slime out of my hair and we laid back on the edge of the pool until I dried off and we started home.

Walking back along the cow path we could hear Brian and them splashing and yelling in Tucker's Pond. Come on, I said, we have to get that rat fucker back. Then we were bellycrawling to where their clothes were hanging over a branch. We had to wait till they all ran in the water, splashing and whooping and not paying attention to the shore. Then I took Brian's pants and his shirt with the cigarettes and I tied them around the biggest rock I could find. I ran to the edge of the dock and yelled, Hey Brian! You shitpecker, Fuck you! and I threw them out into the water where they sank down fast. He started swimming toward us screaming, I'll kill you, you little fuck! but there was no way he could catch us. We booked it back toward the cow path but as we passed the tree with their clothes in it I grabbed Willow's underwear and I took them too.

We ran the whole way to the power lines before we had to stop because of Eddie's asthma so we walked back the rest of the way to Eddie's house and hid in the top of the grain silo where we could see anyone coming. We sat up there for a long time trying to figure out how to hide from Brian the whole rest of the summer. Then we started throwing ears of old corn down, seeing who could land one in the cow trough below. I got six but Eddie only got three. We did that for a while until Eddie started singing, *There's a skeeter on my peter, beat it off,* and we cracked up and forgot all about Brian and the others. By then no one came looking for us, so we decided to climb down because it was hot as a mug up there. On the ladder Eddie asked me about Willow's snatch again but I didn't say anything.

But as we were passing the barn we saw Eddie's sister going in with Brian now dressed in dry clothes so we ducked behind the chicken coop till they were gone. Eddie said, Let's spy on 'em, and even though I was still scared of Brian I said okay and we climbed in a back window and up into the rafters above the hay loft. We saw them down below us and crawled

Eddie's Mom

super quiet along the beam until we were right above them in the shadows. Cheryl was lying in the hay and Brian was kissing her neck with his hand under her shirt. Then she pulled her shirt off and undid her bra and her boobs hung out. Brian started kissing them too and Eddie started giggling so I told him shhh, but he said, They can't hear us, stupid, the cows are right below them, and I knew he was right. You could hear them stamping and snorting and mooing. Then Brian took his clothes off and stood up in front of her. His rod was sticking straight out. She sat up and touched it for a while then pulled off her jeans. She had a big black hairy bush, not light and beautiful like Willow's. Eddie stopped giggling then and we just watched as Brian laid down on top of her. What are they doing? I asked, and Eddie said, They're screwing, stupid. Oh, I said, I knew that, even though I really didn't. I started to get that wobbly feeling again and I had to hold onto the beam so I wouldn't fall off. I wanted to go home. I didn't want to see any more.

Then all of a sudden Eddie stood up in front of me laughing with his pecker in his hand. What are you doing? I said, but he didn't answer, he just yelled out, Hey Cheryl! Hey Brian! and he started to piss on them. Eddie, you miserable little fuck! Cheryl yelled up at him. Fuck you! But Eddie was waving his thing back and forth so they were getting totally soaked. That was totally awesome, so I started laughing too even though I still wanted to leave and I was afraid that Eddie might fall and break his arm again. Brian and Cheryl were grabbing their clothes and trying to get out of the way. Brian was yelling, I'm gonna cut your fucking dick off, you little shit, get down here, and that's when Eddie's mom came in.

She was tending cuts on one of the cows below. She still had a rag stained blue and a jar of salve in her hands when she stepped up into the loft and saw Brian and Cheryl all naked getting pissed on. Gotdamnit! she yelled, You fucking slut, what the hell do you think you're doing up here? Then Brian and Cheryl both forgot about us while they tried to hide their naked bodies from Eddie's mom. They started to put their clothes back on, even with Eddie's piss all over them, but Eddie's mom just tore them away and started slapping at them both. She hit Cheryl hard across the face and Cheryl fell crying in the hay. She slapped Brian across his shoulders as he tried to turn away from her and then she grabbed a broken pitchfork handle and started hitting him and that's when Eddie and I stopped laughing. Brian was blubbering and saying he was sorry, please stop, but she just kept smacking him. Wait till I tell your parents what you've been doing, she yelled, Just wait till I tell 'em! then Brian tried to crawl away but she kept moving after him.

When the beating was over Eddie's mom had us climb down and we were all standing outside in the last light of the afternoon. Now, she said, You got two choices, Brian Mills, you take your whoopin' like a man and stay away from my house and my daughter for the rest of your miserable life, or I'll tell your folks what you were doing in my barn today and I know your daddy'll give you a thrashin' makes mine feel like love. Yes ma'am, Brian said through his swollen face, but as we were all turning away, Brian said real quiet, I'm gonna kill you two little faggots. Then faster than lightning Eddie's mom whirled around and smacked Brian so hard across his mouth that spit shot out of it before he hit the ground. Do you think I'm joshin' you, boy? she said standing over him crawling in the dirt. Do you think to make a mockery of me on my own land? If I hear one word from these two boys, just one word that they've suffered harm under your hand, so help me Jesus, I'll come crawling in your window one night and slice your dirty little pecker right off and feed it to the pigs. Now get the hell offa my land!

Brian got up and limped as fast as he could toward the road. Cheryl ran into the house with just her underpants on and I snuck another look at her bouncing boobs. Eddie and I stood scared and silent in front of his mom in case she decided to hit us too for watching them screw or for not cleaning out the chicken coop but Eddie's mom looked down at Colin's medal hanging crooked outside my torn shirt and her face changed. She knew about the medal because I wore it all the time and she said, Did that boy Brian do this to you? and even though I didn't want to, I started to cry again like a little kid but I couldn't help it. I couldn't get the words out I wanted to say so I just nodded. You poor boy, she said, you've suffered enough without that lowlife picking on you. And then she pulled me in and hugged me. At first I was scared so I pulled away a little but she held me tight. Finally I just let go and let her hold me while I cried. After a while she said, Let's get you inside and see what we can do to fix that chain.

And even though I'm still mad at her for all that stuff she said about Frances and because she made my mother cry at Colin's funeral, I let her take my hand and lead me across the yard like I was six or something. Eddie had a look on his face I couldn't understand but he followed us into the house without saying a word maybe in case she changed her mind and got mad at him for not finishing his chores, but she didn't mention the chicken coop once. She had us sit in the dining room while she fixed the silver chain with pieces of wire she had in a basket and then she gave me and Eddie cherry popsicles that melted down our fingers faster than we could eat them.

Le Machinne
Megan Erickson

～

My child has begun to say the words *Night night, bye bye*.
In the evening, in his crib, he waves me away with them joyfully,
understanding their power, if not their precise meaning.
He knows enough: that I will go, that he will fall asleep alone,
that we will wake up together. I am so pleased
by this little act of bravery I ask him to repeat it again and again
in front of aunts and friends, like it's a joke, instead of the first split
in the almost visible skin binding him and me. He and I. I, he.

This morning he wakes jet-lagged at five a.m., drinks milk
in the navy-blue light. Turns the pages of a book about machines
written in Italian bought to keep him quiet in the airport.
I think of all I do to subdue him: the games, the screens,
the wooden blocks and the plastic light-up ones
when the wooden ones didn't absorb his attention long enough.
When will there be enough quiet for me? When he stops asking
for another song before the lights go out? When I can no longer hold him
in my arms

and hear his breath against my neck? Now he turns the page
and points to *il treno* and *la motocicletta*,
a picture of a big family waving at a car full of children,
says: *Night night. Bye, bye*. I correct him: *Good morning, hello, breakfast time!*
I want to say, *Can't you see they are only just arriving?*
I want to say, anyway, it's we who are transient—
tires and transmission fluid outlast tissue and bone as surely as rock beats
scissors. But he is learning the order of things: how *automobiles* work,
how they are made up of parts that break, how sometimes
they can be put back together again. How they run.
I am learning to watch him go.

The Doors of Perception in Palestine

a series by
Nicholas Karavatos

#7

#8

#4

*each photograph was
captured and edited
with an iPhone 8*

#10

98   *Fourteen Hills*

from

Ganap

a novel by *Liz Iversen*

∼

Liwayway, I have become a prisoner again. There are hundreds of us in one camp, unbathed and dirty, underfed. Everyone around me, mothers and their children, men who must have once been strong, are withered to bones. Grown men weigh only as much as me. They walk around with protruding ribs. In the middle of the day, when the sunlight is strongest, their bodies appear like skeletons in the blinding white light.

Konishi, the commander in charge, has cut our food rations. We get one bowl of *lugaw* per day now, and no meat from outside. The guards hunt caribou for themselves and cook it in the kitchen. The smell hangs thick in the humid air. I close my eyes and I taste it, *chile con carne* with caribou meat in place of beef, as *nanay* made it. But the smell does nothing to ease my hunger. We are starving and the few guards hoard the meat for themselves. They dine and there is laughter, clinking of glasses and scraping of plates. And when the sun sets, they open the door and saunter past with smiling red faces and stuffed bellies. They tell us they have no meat even as the juices drip from their chins.

In the comfort station I had my own bed, but here we sleep on the floor in cramped rooms. There is an American girl in my room, Marisa, and an old woman who reminds me of *nanay*. But she is not *nanay* and this fact is so painful to me that I cannot bear to look at her. She must think I do not like her, that I cannot stand the sight of her sunken-in face, the face of my future should I live to see it. But in fact it is the opposite. Even though I do not know her, I have love for her. Maybe it is that there is no one else here to love. But I see her suffering and feel it with my whole heart.

Marisa says before I arrived, the Japanese fed everyone three meals a day. She says she picked the bugs out from her *lugaw* then, instead of eating them as we do for protein.

Konishi is starving us in the cruelest way. I tell you, Liwayway, he will force starving men, men weighing 100 pounds, to carry 100-pound bags of rice.

He directs them to the cooking shed and they go, hunched over under the weight of the bag that threatens to crush them. And as soon as the rice is stocked he tells them to haul it back. We don't taste a morsel of this rice, the rice that starving men nearly crippled themselves for. He tortures us with its possibility, the anticipation and loss.

Oh, Liwayway! I dream of food, of *sisig* and *lumpia* and crispy *pata*. Even the pleasure of a piece of fruit has become a distant memory. I dream of stumbling upon a hidden grove of trees bursting with ripe bananas. In my sleep, I eat and strip bare the trees until the ground is carpeted in peels. Then I wake to blackness, stomach aching and mouth watering.

I lay on my mat until I can no longer bear it. I get up and shake Marisa awake. Without a word, I grab her wrist and we sneak past the others asleep on the floor, through the courtyard and to the kitchen. To my surprise, there is no guard at the door, but the cupboards and refrigerator are locked. We are so desperate for nourishment we turn to the trash. There, nestled among a pile of scraps are several caribou bones. We pick them out and suck them clean of the remnants they contain.

#

Marisa is convinced the Americans will return, that MacArthur will hold true to his promise and we will be set free. I am not so sure. The radio says nothing of it. Then one day as I am walking in the courtyard, I hear the buzz of planes. It is a sound I have not heard in months, and when I look up three American military planes are passing over the camp. The internees near me stop in their tracks. We turn our faces toward the sky. Dozens of us standing frozen, as if the planes have stopped time. We do not wave our arms or cry out for joy. We have learned not to incite anger in the Japanese guards, who flee from the planes to shelter beneath the trees. But we are fearless, transfixed, hands shielding our squinting eyes against the sun illuminating our passing savior. They have returned, Liwayway! The Americans have returned! I cannot hold back a smile as I rush to tell Marisa. Each internee I pass is smiling too. We lock eyes in silent triumph. For the rest of the day my excitement overrides my hunger. I think not of savory meat or sweet *halo halo*, but of the taste of sea air on my lips. Hope nourishes my body when food cannot.

#

Every day people line up at the fence for the handouts that come from villagers on the outside. Friends and family, even strangers who have not had our misfortune, come to this place to feed us. Sometimes I wonder why we were chosen. Why those on the outside remain free. But I am grateful to them, for sometimes—though I have not seen any face I recognize—someone will pass me through the fence a bit of rice or fish or a ripe mango or guava. I look for you every day, Liwayway.

Today there was a skirmish at the gate. Two men fighting over a handful of fried *camote*. It escalated to violence and a guard broke in. You will never guess the identity of the guard who broke it up. It was our former neighbor, Rodrigo de Guzman!

Remember how Rodrigo de Guzman and *tatay* used to hold meetings in the rice shed? How they and the other guerillas would curse the Japanese and plot to overthrow them? Now our former neighbor is one of them! He stands guard over us, reporting to the Japanese our activities and overheard bits of conversation. He is a traitor, Liwayway, a *Ganap*! I see him and I know he recognizes me, but he will not bring himself to look in my direction. He stares past me, over my head at the crowd, going out of his way to avoid my gaze.

His presence incites a rage I thought I'd left behind at the comfort station. Can you imagine, Liwayway, this man who was like an uncle to us, like a brother to our father—this man who railed with *tatay* against the Japanese has become one of them? I cannot bear the sight of his pig face. He has grown fatter while forcing his own people to starve. He is spineless. He is a coward. I am so filled with hatred I could scream.

I want to talk to Rodrigo, ask him why he's changed. There are other Filipino guards within these walls. Were they bribed with food or money or better living quarters? Maybe they were threatened with death if they refused to follow orders. It is hard for me to imagine, but I wonder what I, too, might have done under similar circumstances. You never know a person, sister, even if you think you do. You never know all the twists and turns of their heart.

#

Sometimes the women who share my room offer me bits of food. The woman who reminds me of *nanay* gives me more than she keeps for herself. I wonder if she is inured to the pain of starvation. She refuses to eat even when I insist, when, mouth watering, I tell her I am not hungry.

Her eyes are turning a cloudy blue, and, though she has never admitted it, I am certain she is losing her ability to see. Sometimes she trips over things even in daylight, and sometimes, though she looks me in the face, it seems she is somehow not seeing me. I want to take care of her, sister, but I can barely take care of myself.

The old woman has an ancient book that she keeps hidden from the guards. I try to read it when she is outside on her daily stroll about camp. "For air," she says before stepping out, but I know the real reason she walks—to eavesdrop on camp gossip, to hear news of what is happening within these walls and on the other side.

I pull the book out from the bag where it is hidden beneath all of her belongings. It is heavier than I expect, its cover made of cracked leather. I wonder how the woman managed to keep it with her all this time, how she had the strength to carry it from wherever she had come. I flip through its yellowed pages, brown at the edges. Beneath the title on each page are a few lines written in a language I do not understand.

The woman takes the book out some evenings after dark and strains to read it by candlelight. Sometimes she closes her eyes and hums or chants and moves her hands around in strange ways. Is she performing magic on herself or on me, or on someone far away? I want to ask. But each time we are together, alone, I open my mouth and it occurs to me that if I speak of the spells, they may lose their power. So I study her face, her body, her hands. She is always the same: the mole on her cheek, the same shade of gray hair, the same wrinkles creasing her forehead as the day before. Still, I cannot shake the feeling that she—her book—has changed something. There is power here. I can feel it, even if I cannot see it.

I tell her about you, Liwayway, in the hopes that her magic—if that's what it is—will bring you to me. I tell her stories about when we were children, about how you were the most beautiful girl in our province. I tell her that you were always the head of your class, that *nanay* and *tatay* said you would achieve great things, that I wanted to be like you but I wasn't. I was too afraid, or too shy, or I lacked your abilities. The old woman listens, sometimes with closed eyes, and sometimes I think she has fallen asleep. But even if she has, it is comforting to have someone to speak to, someone who can hear my memories and, by listening to them, affirm that they are real.

#

One day as I am sitting alone in camp, reading a book the old woman gave me, Rodrigo de Guzman walks past. He walks so close his arm brushes against me. I look up just in time to see a rice cake slip from his hand. It is wrapped in a banana leaf, so when it hits the ground it remains perfectly intact. I gasp when I see it, and I stand up to ask whether it is a gift or if was dropped it by accident. But he moves quickly, is already steps away before I can reach out, and he does not look back.

I bend over and tuck the treat in my pocket. No one is paying attention. Then I slip back to the room I share with the other women. No one is there. I go to the corner of the room and hunch over my treasure to hide it from view. It is sweet and creamy, oozing carmelized sugar. I lift it to my face, am poised to take a bite, when I feel someone's eyes on me.

I turn to look and there is Marisa. Her eyes are wide and hooked on the food in my hand. I turn to the rice cake dripping creamy sweetness, break it in half, and extend her portion to her.

#

Marisa's parents came here as missionaries, but then her father became a guerilla like *tatay*. She doesn't know where here family is now. The Japanese took them away when they brought her here.

She tells me stories about America, about how the homes have indoor plumbing and almost every child goes to school, even the children of poor farmers who need help with the harvest. She tells me about all the stores that hold everything money can buy.

I must go to America. I want to see if the place is truly as wonderful as she says. I want to go to America, and that is why I approached our former neighbor, who was once like a father to us, and begged him to open the prison gate.

Sister, let me tell you about what happened when I approached Rodrigo de Guzman. When I asked him, not in so many words, if he would take pity on me, turn a blind eye and let me escape.

I waited until he was alone.

"Rodrigo," I said. "Rodrigo, it's me, Malaya."

He did not look at me, and I began to wonder what was real, if he was really our former neighbor, or if I did not exist.

"Rodrigo," I said again but he just gripped the rifle in his hands, looking out at the sea of faces in the camp. He was wearing a Japanese army uniform, and I wondered how long he had been one of them.

What happens when a person becomes a traitor? Do they forget who they were and everything they once knew, including their own neighbors? Or does the guilt consume them? Is every moment, every breath, a dull ache and a contradiction of their soul?

I wanted to believe that Rodrigo de Guzman remembered me, that when he saw me here, when he stood guard over me and the hundreds of other Filipinos in this place, that he yearned for that part of himself that once fought for freedom against the Japanese. I hoped that if he were not brave enough to lead a rebellion here, on the inside, as he had done before, that he might still be swayed to serve his former goal in a small way by letting me and Marisa escape. That is what I implored him to do, when we were alone and out of earshot. I walked up to our former neighbor and I asked if he would please, when night fell, look the other way and let us be free.

Liwayway, he did not even look at my face as he struck it with his gun. I fell to the ground and Rodrigo de Guzman walked away.

Marisa later told me the old woman went to grab her as I lay there. She and the woman draped my arms around their shoulders and dragged me to my room. Marisa sat with me, talking and stroking my hair, wiping my face with a wet cloth. I did not wake up for hours.

What kind of a world is this, sister, when someone who once loved you could turn away from you for no reason? I did nothing to make our neighbor hate me, and yet he might have killed me. I didn't know I could still be surprised by the evil that exists in the world. That it should arise so startlingly, even in places where we have known kindness and love. I hope, sister, that you have not been taught these lessons as I have, that the world still retains its beauty and brings happiness to you.

The Boy Who Lives In Dreams
Saúl Hernández

Dreams run in my family. In mine I
    nail water to the wall, it runs down

my hands and splashes at my feet, leaks
    into the cracks of the wood floor. In

the morning I wash my face, water
    goes down my elbows and

drips. I hear the water in the sink ask
    me: *I need to know your*

dreams. Apá fights at night, I can hear
    him toss and groan. He knows where

they will take him: to see his brother
    drown. I take sleeping pills sometimes,

I become heavy enough to not
    dream. Like when Amá puts Valium pills in her

mouth, keeping her father from telling her:
    why didn't you come bury me? When it rains

I have to remember I'm awake, not dreaming.
    Water remembers its path, always forming

the same stream in the same direction like
    the way my body waits at night:

always still. I sweat out the night,
>   I can hear wet drops slam against the floor. I

get up, open the cracks of the wood floor,
>   take a shovel, scoop up all the water that has leaked

through, toss it out. Underneath all the layers
>   of water I find my uncle's mouth, it tells me:

I'm not going to hurt you. Then his *shhh* floods me.
>   In the morning water leaks into my pillows.

Performance Notes
Patrick Kindig

∼

My boyfriend, a master's student in saxophone performance, has been chosen to perform Alexander Glazunov's saxophone concerto in concert. His name was chosen at random from a pool of applicants, but good things just seem to happen to him. He will memorize the piece and play it before an audience with an orchestra at his back.

He is both classically handsome and very talented. He will be the center of attention.

,

When I first see my boyfriend perform the Glazunov, he is wearing a tee shirt. I can see the muscles of his forearms flex each time he presses a key. It is winter break and we have snuck into an empty recital hall and every noise he makes makes an echo, even his breath.

I am used to his body's gestures. I have seen him perform in ensembles, in his quartet. I am used to seeing him dip and sway and lean into phrases as if he is walking into a heavy wind. But I have never seen him perform in this kind of context before, never watched him move alongside the movements of a piece I recognize.

Tonight I notice things.

For example, during the concerto's first virtuosic run, he braces himself. He plants his feet beneath his shoulders and stops his chest from moving. It is a hero's pose, the pose of a man receiving an athletic award, and it carries him through the tonal acrobatics of the moment. And yet when the run returns later in the piece, he is supremely nonchalant. He bends at the hip and pivots to the left, letting the notes roll down him like water.

For another, his eyes have distinct ways of wandering. With no music to read, they look at the balcony above my head. But when a note is sharp, they lift, explore the ceiling. They rise with the pitch of the saxophone. And when, near the end, the music grows sweeping, spiraling outward into arpeggio after arpeggio, both his body and his eyes become untethered, roving the stage with abandon.

When, after finishing, he asks me what I noticed, I tell him this.

The movements are not conscious or intentional, he says, but he knows he makes them. He is not surprised.

,

Concerti, my boyfriend tells me, traditionally revolve around one of two figures: the innate hero, who enters the world already triumphant, or the processual hero, who only triumphs after a long struggle. The piece that takes the innate hero as a model is virtuosic, about demonstrating skill; the piece that models itself after the processual hero is about thematic development. One is about being heroic, the other about becoming so.

Glazunov's saxophone, he says, is a processual hero. Unlike the violin in Paganini's first concerto, which he calls *flashy*, Glazunov's saxophone exhibits restraint, more interested in developing a theme than in showing off its range. The music is difficult but it is unassumingly so, a piece that invites prolonged study.

Every time he plays it, he says, the Glazunov is hard. It never becomes easier.

,

Between rehearsals, we work out together. At the gym I see his body glisten in the fluorescent lights, grow stronger. I see it becoming heroic.

When he does bicep curls, he does them slowly. He does squats on the squat machine and does not lock his knees once. He uses the elliptical for half an hour, never breaking a sweat.

His form on every machine is impeccable.

,

Before you memorize, my boyfriend tells me a week before the concert, you need to know yourself. You need to know what your primary mode of remembering is. Some people are visual, some aural. His primary mode, he says, is feeling. He is *very kinesthetic*. It is difficult for him to recall the sound of a concerto, but his muscles remember. This is how he knows the Glazunov.

,

A century ago, it was common practice for performers to hypnotize themselves. They used autosuggestion to enter trance states, remove the fallible conscious mind from the equation. Unselfconsciousness was thought to be the source of grace, of natural movement, of liveness.

I tell my boyfriend this, that turn-of-the-century performers handled their minds and bodies with a light touch. *Exactly*, he says. *Exactly*.

,

When I see my boyfriend perform the Glazunov in concert, it is a different experience.

He stands onstage not in a tee shirt but in a suit coat, forearms hidden from view. The recital hall is dark according to convention, the stage lit. Before he begins he looks into the darkness and bows, nods to the conductor. Then he begins.

The sound of his saxophone is softer than it was before, smoother and warmer. And yet it is a shock against the even softer sound of the orchestra. The saxophone is a modern instrument and the string orchestra is not. The saxophone solicits attention. It is like a splash of red on a classical painting.

My boyfriend is surrounded by other musicians today but he is still what draws the eye. Behind him, the cellists and violinists raise and lower their bows, give the impression of movement. But it is my boyfriend and his saxophone that stand out, a flash of gold in front of the orchestra's muted black. He is in the foreground and the orchestra is in the background, is the background. It is his gestures that the audience is compelled to watch.

In concert, I realize, his gestural strategy has changed. If, when I last saw him play the Glazunov, his movements were heroic, exuded strength, today they are elegant, refined and graceful. Gone are the bulging biceps, the hips squared off. Gone even are the wandering eyes. Now his movements, like the processual hero's, are smooth, restrained. He moves his body fluidly, as if caught in a breeze.

After the concert, a girl in the audience tells him he makes performing look *effortless*. He tells her it takes a lot of work to make it look that way. He also tells her this is his favorite compliment to receive.

,

This is, in the end, only one of performance's many paradoxes. Performing involves the body at both its most mechanical and its most vital. It requires a training of muscle, a kinetic learning that is almost entirely unconscious. And yet it is also an intensely revelatory experience, one that allows an audience to glimpse something like a performer's soul. Performance knits mind to body, intention to expression. It enacts a kind of transubstantiation, making of the body's many composite parts a sign.

,

Yet if my boyfriend's body is a sign, it is an unstable one. Just as it rocks itself back and forth onstage, so, too, does it rock between affective and aesthetic meanings, between the kinds of impressions it conveys to an audience. If, on the one hand, it can embody heroic power, it can also, on the other, move with utter grace. It is capable of oscillating between strength and gentleness, freedom and control, speaking to the audience in a language more felt than understood. Each gesture describes his body anew, and his body's contours are constantly changing.

The evening after the Glazunov performance, his body continues to change. We go to bed together and it is just the two of us, no saxophones, no suitcoats, no rapt audience attending. My boyfriend's muscles are exposed but this time they are tender, more yielding, like the machinery that moves sunflowers. I enter him and for a time the shapes of our bodies are inseparable, become one wet shape imprinting itself on the sheets. Then we separate and lie back and fall asleep, release our bodies to their unconscious metabolic tasks, to their unconscious dreamwork.

If we touch each other in the night, we may enter each other's dreams. If we dream in the night, we may not remember come morning.

Magic in the Hiss
Ashleigh A. Allen

~

Sun rises against the will and trumpets have made their way to the mouths of children again. The cars turn down the residential street a mile away at 7 a.m., wave their lights through the trees like Cheshire judgment. I wig in and out. Leave the scab on my face to avoid scarring. The daffodils look like plastic this year; so far away from what I can put in my body. Are you listening? The hyacinths seem calm but will be bitter when the April snow arrives later today. They look at me; fireworks that never dim, and it'd be excess or I'd be bear if I wasn't born for the April cause. I enlisted in life for this. To be here. Took the king's shilling. Fingered the icing off the edge of the cake before I knew what we were celebrating. To what purpose, death? To what law, fence? Men have drawn equations here where there used to be just sand. They plucked wings from birds to wipe their asses. In a room of glory who loses their bowels first? In a field I find a swing; soar for only a few minutes. Even the wind dies sometimes. Somewhere within me there is a slice of darkness unknowable. I spend each day covering it with smut and dog bark, mulch and song. I lean away from the silent crevice. My back, when naked, feels like the topography of West Virginia. Nighttime cigarettes and wakeful mind curls. An appreciation for windows, wet road, and rubber tires. Everything reminds me of battle, my nail polished hands land bright red on the chests of friends. Shush lovers to their dreams. Pussy willows haunt the season with their aching. Jesus will die this week and no one places bets on him; no one but me. This year he just dies, end of cycle. No telephones, just curtains. Pure starts and high tides. We live in a place where we die once for the worms but twice in the eyes. There is no intended destination of fear or fire. Medicine heroes through our bodies like soldiers full of chapel verse and gun marrow. This modern life is lonely, honey. I embrace the complex sky, the flute in the handkerchief. The stripes of my ghosts leap. It doesn't mean a damn thing. The women oil each other, and it's more beautiful than I could have imagined. Hearts glisten.

Mrs. D'Souza's Mango Tree
Hema Padhu

~

The Muskas wanted to steal mangoes from Mrs. D'Souza's tree not because they were sweeter or bigger but because no one liked Mrs. D'Souza. A dour woman, she was rumored to hate children, a reputation she further substantiated by refusing to return the many errant cricket balls that had missed their mark and ended up in her garden. Stealing her mangoes was a perfect way to end their summer adventures and a thrilling story to take back to school. A story that could hold its own against the stories of privileged kids returning from holidays at some remote hill station where they rode a Yak or went up the mountain on a ski lift.

The Muskas, an unfortunate reduction of their gang's name from the original Musketeers, planned to meet at their usual spot, under the neem tree behind Sri's house and Aarthi didn't want to be late. She was looking forward to setting her tree-climbing record to fifteen, four more than she'd climbed last year. Sri, the self-appointed and unchallenged leader of the Muskas, held the record for the most trees climbed in a summer, nineteen. At twelve, Aarthi was slightly built, her body a treacherous terrain erupting with new and unpleasant discoveries that alarmed her. Many girls her age had already had their first period, and every morning Aarthi awoke with anticipation and dread wondering if this would be the day she'd become a *big girl*, as her grandmother liked to say. She longed to be a part of that exclusive club of *big girls* who huddled together at school giggling and talking in hushed whispers. But she feared her tree-climbing days would swiftly come to an end. The other girls who used to climb with her had stopped after they became *big girls*.

Before the Muskas' meeting, Aarthi stopped at Kittu's mobile *istri* stand to drop off a bundle of her mother's sarees and blouses for ironing. The *istri* stand stood outside the D'Souza's compound wall, under the shade of their mango tree. Kittu was cleaning out day-old charcoal from the iron box he'd soon fill with fresh hot coals. Aarthi handed the bundle to Kittu, who nodded and threw it on top of the growing pile of clothes he'd iron that day. Kittu couldn't speak, so he signaled with his hands and made grunting noises that somehow everyone understood. The generally circulated story was that someone had cut his tongue out—reportedly his father. He'd lied about stealing sweets from a shop during Diwali because his father couldn't afford to buy him any. But Aarthi felt this was a story adults had made up to stop children from lying or stealing. Kittu's son, Chinna Kittu (Little Kittu because no one knew his real name) was pumping water from a nearby hand pump. The boy was slight and he jumped to grab the rusted handle of the water pump that flew up like a persistent question mark immediately after it was brought down. He threw all his weight behind it to fill the metal bucket with a flush of muddy water. Aarthi told him to step aside.

—We are going to climb the tree tomorrow. Are you ready? she asked, pumping fast.

He nodded, sniffling, and wiping his nose on his cotton shirt sleeve, a hand-me-down from Aarthi. His threadbare shorts were a size too big and a coir rope served as a makeshift belt. His shoulder blades stuck out like bat wings and his hair hadn't seen water or a comb for days. Aarthi spotted lice eggs in the dark strands.

—Hhhhhow mmmany mangoes can wwe ggget, *Akka*? he asked, fear and excitement brightened his eyes.

Aarthi had met Chinna Kittu when her mother had moved them to Mayilai Lane five years ago after her father's death. He'd knocked on their door one evening to return their ironed clothes wearing a faded, moth-holed, sleeveless vest. His eyes were like two pieces of charcoal in his dreamy, oval face. Giving her a big, toothy grin, he called her *Akka*. Aarthi was only seven then and no one had ever called her "big sister". When her grandmother told her that he didn't have a mother and Kittu was all he had, she'd felt an immediate kinship with him.

—The tree had a dozen ripe mangoes when we last counted. Don't be afraid. Stay close to me and you'll be fine, she whispered.

He smiled. His front tooth was missing but the rest were surprisingly bright despite using ground charcoal as toothpaste and his forefinger for a brush. Chinna Kittu didn't go to school. At ten, he was just two years younger than Aarthi but he could barely read and write. Most of the time he was staring into space with an odd, beatific smile and Aarthi couldn't tell if he was dreaming, thinking, or simply vacant. He said little, intuiting that his speech was an imposition, and still the kids made fun of his stutter. But whenever he saw Aarthi his face burst open like a sparkler on Diwali night. He'd wait for her by the streetlamp every evening, beaming and waving when he saw her step out of the school bus. She'd save him some of her lunch and the joy with which he ate these scraps—a piece of a cheese sandwich, a slice of apple, or a lemon pickle (his favorite), gave Aarthi something to look forward to after school.

Yesterday, Chinna Kittu had told her he'd never tasted a ripe mango, astonishing Aarthi who was eating two a day at the peak of summer. Her father had taught her how to pick out the ripe ones. Their orange-gold color, the gentle give of the fruit when pressed lightly, the sweet smell at the stem's end. He told her the juiciest part of the mango was attached to seed and he'd always save the seed for her. She thought about the mango milkshake she'd had for breakfast. Chinna Kutti had probably never tasted a milkshake in his life. Aarthi decided immediately that he would be part of the Muskas final mango heist and promised him two mangoes.

The neem tree behind Sri's home used to belong to a house that was demolished. The land was contested and therefore neglected, overrun with weeds and wild shrubbery. A perfect place for the Muskas to plan their adventures. When Aarthi arrived, Sri was sitting on the boulder, his throne from which he directed the meeting. He'd just turned fourteen and had gained two inches in height this summer. Heat boils erupted on his arms and neck: proof he ate more mangoes than anyone else in the group. He wore them proudly, like medals he'd won at sports day. He knew that girls were both repulsed and strangely fascinated by them. It only added to his popularity.

—It's time for the last summer adventure of the Muskas. His voice crackled and his Adam's apple bobbed as he spoke. —Let's go over the plan. Bala and I will climb the D'Souza tree. Aarthi and Kris will collect the mangoes.

Kris (short for Krishna) nodded, his eyes slightly crossed behind his metal-framed glasses. They had broken after his fall from the last climb and were held together with black tape. A year younger than Sri and Bala, he'd finally entered the coveted teen years this summer and had started shaving in secret to encourage facial hair. Privately, he worried he'd stop growing and that Aarthi, who at twelve was already five foot four, might shoot past him, never giving him a chance.

—I can climb too, Aarthi said. —I need to beat my last year's tree-climbing record.

—You and your tree-climbing record, Bala rolled his eyes. He was not looking at Aarthi but at some distant point over her left shoulder. He was sitting on a low branch of the neem tree as if he were riding a horse. Bala avoided all girls, ducking behind stairwells and hugging walls to prevent the slightest, most accidental brush with the giggling girls at school. That summer, Aarthi, all of a sudden started despising him and writing about him in her journal.

—Climbing the D'Souza tree is no joke, *di*, Sri added in that superior voice he used to speak to girls. Aarthi hated that he called all girls, *di*. A crude reduction of her gender. —It's for boys. And, we need you and Kris to catch the mangoes.

Aarthi pulled Chinna Kittu forward. He was standing behind her this entire time and no one had noticed. —He's going to help Kris.

Sri snickered, shaking his head. —No way, *di*. He can't steal mangoes to save his life. He'll get us all into trouble. He tossed a small pebble at Chinna Kittu, shouting, —Catch! It sailed past him as he ducked.

—See, Sri said. —He's hopeless, *di*. Bala and Kris laughed. Kris louder because he didn't want to miss this opportunity to be Aarthi's partner in crime.

—He has never had a mango. Aarthi said. —How many have you eaten this summer?

—So give him a mango, *di*. From your kitchen.

—It's not the same thing, is it?

Aarthi was certain nothing in this world quite matched the bursting sweetness of a ripe mango, except, a *stolen* ripe mango. The thrill of stealing a mango added to its sweetness and nothing would match the special joy of stealing from Mrs. D'Souza. The woman held a particular kind of contempt for Chinna Kittu, the kind that is reserved for a failed experiment. Taking pity on the boy, she had attempted to tutor him. Buying him books and pencils, spending an hour a day teaching him to read and write. But her hectoring ways only intimidated him and his stutter worsened. Finally, Kittu rescued him saying that he needed his help to run the *istri* stand. To punish both the Father and Son, Mrs. D'Souza treated Chinna Kittu like an errand boy, never paying him for the work he did. Once, Aarthi had witnessed her grabbing him by the ear and shaking him roughly when he accidentally over-starched Mr. D'Souza's shirt. Having spent her summer reading *Great Expectations* and *Adventures of Huckleberry Finn*, Aarthi had a keen understanding of the concept of justice. Including Chinna Kittu in this final mango theft of the summer would be a small but satisfying way to pay that woman back for her unkindness.

Aarthi gave Bala and Kris a beseeching look. Kris nodded but Bala chewed on a neem twig, avoiding her gaze. She had expected this. The boys could easily get the mangoes without her help. She had come prepared.

—I'll give you my Burundi stamp, she said.

Sri almost fell off his boulder. Bala, briefly forgetting his aversion to girls, stared at Aarthi while simultaneously fighting the anxiety that this stamp might put Sri's collection ahead of his.

Aarthi felt a small jolt of joy. She had their attention. The stamp of Burundi belonged to her father's stamp collection. Her mother didn't know if her father had ever been to Burundi but she imagined he had. She imagined each stamp in his collection came from places he'd flown to as a pilot: Tanzania, Peru, Burundi, Scotland. This particular stamp was yellow with a black border and a white-tailed gnu was grazing in the jungles of Burundi. The boys had coveted it, offering their stamps as a trade but she had refused.

—Is this a trade? Sri frowned with suspicion.

—No. I will give it to you if you let Chinna Kutti join us.

Sri shook his head. —Are you crazy, *di*? Are you seriously trading the Burundi stamp so this stuttering idiot can eat a mango? They all stared at Chinna Kutti who stood by Aarthi, grinning.

—Don't call him that! Aarthi shouted. —Will you let him join or what?

She fingered the outline of the Burundi stamp in her shirt pocket. What kind of an *Akka* would she be if she couldn't sacrifice a stamp so her little brother could eat a mango?

The boys huddled around the boulder to discuss her proposition. Aarthi could see Sri was convincing the other two boys. Later she learned that he had offered his Belgium stamp to Bala and an extra mango to Kris to buy their acceptance.

Finally, Sri turned to Aarthi. —Alright, he can join but on one condition. He will follow Kris's orders. Kris pushed his glasses up his nose and thrust his thin chest forward.

—Do you have the stamp, *di*? Sri asked, jumping off the boulder.

Aarthi took it from her shirt pocket, and they huddled around her to admire it. After a few seconds she put it back and said coolly, —I will give it to you tomorrow afternoon when we climb the D'Souzas' tree.

Mr. and Mrs. D'Souza's home had once been a palatial colonial home built in the British era but over time sections had been sold off until just a modest portion remained. Still, compared to the other houses on that street, it was luxurious. Three front rooms of the home had been converted into a typing institute. In the early mornings, between six and nine, one could hear the loud clacking of keys as the typewriter carriages shuddered back and forth as students practiced. Mr. D'Souza, originally from Goa, had moved to Madras and married into money. He now managed the institute that belonged to his wife's family. In their wedding photograph, hanging in the front room fitted with Remington typewriters, Mrs. D'Souza was a shy bride, dressed in white lace, with high cheekbones and lips like a flower petal. She bore little resemblance to the overweight washed-out woman who lived there now, always in a faded housecoat, smelling faintly of chicken marrow and sour milk. She was severely nearsighted but refused to wear glasses so her perpetual squint made her appear more scornful. The institute was closed from noon to four. After lunch, Mr. D'Souza cleaned and oiled the typewriters while Mrs. D'Souza napped.

Aarthi and the boys gathered at the D'Souzas' back entrance at one. The heavy wooden gate that opened into Mylai Lane was locked. Kittu, after his lunch at the dosa stand, had fallen into a temporary food coma, presenting the Muskas with the perfect opportunity to execute their plan.

Sri turned to Aarthi, extending his hand, and she knew it was time. He kissed the stamp with a loud smack before pocketing it. Sri, Bala, and Aarthi would climb over the D'Souza compound wall. After they plucked the mangoes, they'd throw them over the wall to Kris and Chinna Kittu. Kris, taking his supervisory role seriously, positioned Chinna Kittu on one end of the compound wall and himself at the other. He instructed the boy on how to run back to catch the mangoes when they came flying over the wall.

—Like yyyyou catch a ccccrriket ball? Chinna Kittu asked, and Kris nodded. Chinna Kittu was never invited to join a game of street cricket but he loved to watch. Occasionally, if no one else was available, he'd be asked to keep score which he invariably mixed up.

—If you hear any trouble just run with the mangoes in the direction of the Neem tree, Aarthi said. —A bucket is wedged in between the bushes. Toss the mangoes in the bucket and keep running. Got it?

Chinna Kittu nodded, tightening the coir rope holding up his shorts.

Sri was the first to climb. Like a langur monkey, he scaled the compound wall wedging his foot between the broken bricks. Bala and Aarthi followed. Azalea bushes lined the D'Souzas' garden wall. A bucket filled with cricket balls stood next to a hand pump dripping water.

Sri directed them toward a cluster of ripe Banganapalli mangoes. —Remember our rule. We only pick the really ripe ones.

Bala, a strong and fast climber, went for the top branches. Aarthi took the branches to the side. Although these weren't as high, the mangoes were trickier to reach. She lay flat on her chest and crawled forward grasping the branch with both hands and feet like a chameleon. She checked for ripeness and picked two, tossing the mangoes over the wall in Kris's direction. He caught them. Two more mangoes sailed past the other side of the wall, landing with a thud. Chinna Kittu had missed them. Bala, sitting on the branch above her, rolled his eyes. His shirt hitched up, revealing a narrow band of dark hair climbing up his navel. Aarthi quickly looked away, suffused with a warm feeling entirely foreign to her. Sri, the most experienced at this, had picked three large ones. He tossed them to Kris. They had taken seven mangoes. Sri was reaching for two more when the french doors creaked open. Bala, closest to the wall, was the first to react. He jumped, landing on the other side, quiet as a cat. Sri waited, mango in hand, crouching behind a thatch of leaves, his eyes on the french door. It was Mrs. D'Souza. She must've heard the thud of mangoes Chinna Kittu had missed.

—Who's there? Mrs. D'Souza said sharply. Aarthi knew that the woman was too far from the compound wall and too nearsighted to see them. She carefully swung from the branch until she dropped gently behind the Azalea bushes. At the same time, Sri made a break for it hauling himself over the wall. The movement caught Mrs. D'Souza's attention and she shouted, — Aaah! Thieves! Thieves! Stealing mangoes from my tree. She was wearing her signature housecoat. Purple rollers covered her hair. For a woman her size, she moved quickly and was at the wooden gate faster than anyone could have anticipated.

—I saw you, you rascal! she yelled, squinting hard and opening the gate. The boys scrambled in the direction of the neem tree, escaping from sight.

Except for Chinna Kittu who stood petrified, a mango in each hand.

—Ah, *thiruttu* rascal! Mrs. D'Souza hissed, her gravelly voice rising above the quiet afternoon lull. She grabbed Chinna Kittu by his collar, focussing her nearsighted gaze on him. —How dare you climb my mango tree, you ungrateful rascal, she hissed. —Where's your father?

Crouching in the bushes, Aarthi slapped her forehead. She inched her way along the garden's back wall, hiding behind a rhododendron bush to get a better view. She could see Kittu stirring from his nap. He sat up and blinked, trying to make sense of Mrs. D'Souza standing before him like an apparition.

—Is this how you raise your boy? she shouted, spit flying from her mouth.
—I allowed you to park your *istri* stand at my back door, you ungrateful wretch.

Kittu seeing his son dangling from Mrs. D'Souza's fingers, mango in each hand, caught on and vaulted into action. Grabbing Chinna Kittu by the ear, he dragged him over to the *istri* cart raining blows on him. The boy cowered, shielding his head with his arms.

Aarthi watched through the branches of the rhododendron bush feeling both helpless and angry at Chinna Kittu for not getting away. Then it occurred to her that he might have been waiting for her. She had told him to stick close to her, his *Akka*. She was immobilized by a sudden feeling of lightheadedness.

Mrs. D'Souza, having reclaimed the two mangoes that would have otherwise rotted away on her tree, stood watching, lips pursed as Kittu, grunting and cawing, punished his son. Aarthi, seeing the satisfaction on the woman's face, felt a renewed hatred for her. Chinna Kittu, cornered between the bundles of clothing and the *istri* cart, had no escape route. He was yelping like a kicked dog. Aarthi, unable to bear it, decided to take the blame and rose from her hiding spot. A scream, high-pitched and tortured, rang out. Mrs. D'Souza dropped the mangoes. They rolled into a nearby gutter.

Kittu had thrust his son's hand into the iron box filled with hot coals.

That night, Aarthi couldn't sleep. Every time she closed her eyes, she could hear his scream. His dirty face streaked with tears, his right hand charred red and black, the air stinging with the smell of burnt flesh. She was overcome with guilt. As *Akkas* go, she had failed him. She had confessed tearily to her mother, a nurse at the general hospital, who had attended to Chinna Kittu's hand. Aarthi's evident remorse kept her mother from scolding her but she chastised Kittu. He was lucky it wasn't third-degree burns, she told him, instructing him to change his son's bandages every two days.

When the Muskas gathered behind Sri's house the next day, Aarthi narrated what had happened.

—That witch, Sri said flinging a stone in the direction of the D'Souzas' home.

Bala cleared his throat and said, —I don't understand why he just stood there. Why didn't he run? He was looking straight at Aarthi and she flushed.

—He's stupid, Sri mumbled. —That's why.

—Poor boy. Maybe we should give him all our mangoes, Kris said looking at Aarthi, hoping for her approval. When she smiled, he hitched up his shorts and declared that Sri should probably return Aarthi's stamp too.

Sri, worried he might lose his stamp, put a conciliatory arm around Kris. —Good idea, let's give all the mangoes to Chinna Kittu.

Kittu, barred from parking his cart behind the D'Souzas' home, had relocated to the next street over. His eyes narrowed when he saw the four of them approaching.

—We only want to see him, Kittu. No trouble, I promise, Aarthi said.

Chinna Kittu was sitting on a three-legged stool drawing circles in the dirt with a stick. With his right hand bandaged, he couldn't be of much help to Kittu. He grinned when he saw Aarthi and she blinked back tears.

—Does it hurt? she asked, crouching beside him. He shrugged.

—We brought you something, she said. Sri handed him a bag with half a dozen mangoes.

Chinna Kittu gaped. —For me? he asked, and Sri nodded.

—All of it? he asked. They nodded.

Chinna Kittu wiped his left hand on his shirt. He picked up a ripe orange mango and stared at it as if it were a slab of gold. Then he sank his teeth into it. A dribble of bright juice ran down his chin.

They all watched as he chewed and spat out the skin. He swallowed. —I don't like it.

—What? Aarthi couldn't believe her ears. —Take another bite. Maybe that one was bad, she urged. They nodded, watching him intently. He took another bite. More chewing and spitting.

—No, I don't like it. It's too sweet.

He wiped his chin on his shirt sleeve and offered the half-eaten, dripping mango back to Sri whose expression shifted from munificence to outrage.

As they walked back to Mayilai Lane, Sri kicked a stone on the sidewalk sending it skittering into the gutter. —What an idiot. Wasted a good, juicy mango. I picked that one.

—Who doesn't like mangoes? Bala said, shaking his head.

—Aarthi, Kris said, sidling up to her. —Did you notice that Chinna Kittu didn't stammer when he spoke?

Aarthi fought the disappointment of losing her favorite stamp for a wasted effort. But her disappointment would be alleviated later that evening when her period arrived, copiously and unexpectedly. No one could tell whether it was the shock of getting his hand broiled or getting caught by Mrs. D'Souza that did it, but Chinna Kittu never stammered again. With time his hand healed, but a network of scars rippled across his right palm.

∽

Years later, Aarthi, now living in LA after her divorce, went to spend some time in her hometown. It had changed beyond recognition. It was no longer Madras, and she couldn't bring herself to accept the city's new name: Chennai. Her school grounds, once lush with big trees and gardens were crammed with buildings that imprisoned over seventy kids in a class. Her childhood home had been transformed into flats, just like every other home in the neighborhood. But Mayilai Lane was still there, narrower and seedier than Aarthi remembered it.

Mr. D'Souza, she learned, had moved back to Goa. His wife left to visit her sister in Perth and never returned. Gossip had it that a young Jain girl who received private tuition lessons from Mr. D'Souza during his wife's nap time was to be blamed. Mr. D'Souza had been quite content to run the institute alone until computers were decidedly the future, and the kids stopped coming altogether. He couldn't sell the Remingtons until someone suggested he try eBay. Eventually, he sold the house to a land developer who put up an eight-unit flat in its place after chopping down the mango tree.

Aarthi's inquiries about Chinna Kittu led her to an ironing and sewing shop just three streets away from where they'd grown up. She walked in one afternoon and asked for him. A small, dusky woman said no one with that name worked there. That's when Aarthi learned his real name: Ashok. The woman was his wife. They lived above the shop in a modest one-bedroom flat, but it was a far cry from the *istri* cart where he used to sleep as a child. When Ashok called her *Akka*, folding his hands in front of him respectfully, her eyes welled up. She wanted to hug him, but she was aware of his wife standing by him, twisting the ends of her saree. Their flat was small but tidy. Ashok's wife disappeared inside to warm up some *bajjis*. Aarthi sipped coffee from a tumbler and listened while Ashok spoke with pride about sending their five-year-old son to school and his plans for expanding the shop he co-owned with his wife.

—Are you well, *Akka*? he asked her finally.

Aarthi's life was at the lowest point she could remember. The man she had fallen hard for, an investment banker, had turned out to be an unscrupulous coward. He had wiped out their life savings after a series of poor investment decisions and skipped town. Her career as a lawyer working eighty-hour weeks had drained her vital energy just like her husband had drained her bank account. Looking at Ashok's earnest face she couldn't bring herself to admit the truth. She had never been more lost in her life.

She smiled and looked at the floor. —Do you still hate mangoes? she asked. He nodded.

The mangoes Aarthi had in LA were from Mexico or Hawaii, and the firm fruit neither dripped juicily down her fingers nor equaled the taste and texture of the fruits of her childhood. Her summers of eating stolen mangoes with the Muskas, sitting under the neem tree, retelling the story of the climb, revising and incorporating each other's hazy points of view, showing off their scraped knees and elbows, all the while sucking the juices out of the mangoes as it dripped down their hands, represented an effortless pleasure that she couldn't find in her present life.

She asked him if he knew what had happened to the gang. She had lost contact with all but one, Kris. He'd friended her on Facebook years ago.

—Sriram Sir drops off his clothes for ironing every week or so, he said.

Aarthi was surprised that he called Sri 'Sir'. Then she saw in his eyes what she had fought so hard to ignore when she was a girl. He belonged to a different world. He had lived on the street most of his life, slept on the mobile *istri* cart, and survived by eating scraps and charitable handouts. It struck her then that he might have called her *Akka* as a sign of respect. It was *she* who had wanted to be his big sister, his family. He climbed that mango tree not because he wanted to taste mangoes but because *she* had wanted him to. He would have done anything for her because he understood that his fate depended on the kindness or cruelty of people like Aarthi.

—How is your hand?

He extended his right hand, palm facing up. There were no scars. Just the lines of fortune and fate one sees on any hand. He smiled and his teeth, still bright, shone under his neatly trimmed mustache. For a moment, she saw the Chinna Kittu of her childhood, the purity was still there, but the helplessness was gone. Was it ever there? Had she just imagined it? It occurred to her then that he might have found happiness. The kind that was so incandescent, it had the power to chase away the ghosts of his past. Or maybe he always possessed a kind of simple joy. The kind she'd spent all her life chasing.

Archaeology
Jacques Denault

~

The soil is firm, held together by grass, and roots which twist and knot so that I can't be sure which tree they belong to. Blisters are beginning to form on my hands, my fingers curled from gripping the shovel too tightly.

Finally, I strike stone, the remains of a wall, of foundation, of a house. I follow the line, clipping the encroaching roots where I can. Inside the frame I find nails, used for building, for roofing, for furniture, each bent and coated in black rust. I find a pot and pan, brick from what had once been a chimney. I am standing in a kitchen, in the home of someone whose name no one wrote down.

Dolabela Engineer
Guilherme Bergamini

mineral pigment on cotton paper
(from digital photograph)
90 cm × 60 cm

mineral pigment on cotton paper (from digital photograph)
90 cm × 60 cm

Fusca Red *(above)*
Guilherme Bergamini

Check Point Wall #1
Nicholas Karavatos

digital photograph captured &
edited with an iPhone 8

Fourteen Hills

Palinode
B.P. Sutton
2022 Stacy Doris Memorial Poetry Award recipient

❧

‡

sorry thought wrong was wrong scissel our poult rinded themselves to scissel & each our nextborns born unordered less a mouth a draft of bones little said how they began apart less how they knew to drop to scree or loess still young enough to know their form from milk know enough to gum dirt to tell bones

‡

nothing set in the telling bones some years some said some said more not entirely true not entirely unwanted but when born not entirely body no auric dialtone minimal scaffolding what was them simply was born left gave up gave themselves to themselves & dismantled found only a dowsing rod for each we read but no thing declared from sky no thing given from ground no harmonics no ague but some runnel pulleyed light woke to the land milked empty

‡

opened to the milk of animal we lost ourselves in ceremony toothed buckram soaked grain between our teeth yet went unanswered nothing each stalk planted ingrown plaited the next season a season of brined rain a feral season a season noonlight pulled in by hawsers a season we gave birth mouths of gull tongues we dropped to scree filled our jowls in hunger stones even prayed for sacrifice left roadside only grisaille fattened alpenglow again again

‡

not alpenglow andirons empty drought clithral scattershot read each passing hackle read each passing rictus allowed what children left what children ours to remain drafts allowed them this to whichever pattern of ruminants first circled allowed them carried in the water of their bodies held safely safely we said their bodies this prayer

‡

a prayer swallowed until body come water come safety no hum of tongue strained back to mouth no bones strained back to learned form gracious machinery slow mechanics easier to say not unwanted not given birthed themselves off elsewhere distal wandering some unfinished penitence worth but not repented

‡

worthy but not repenting no visions
came no godoffered reason we woke
palms of handpan palms of galena
unordered echo of house a wrung-out
altar each promised newborn dropseed
floorboard adder stone nailed to poplar

‡

said dropseed but nude baleen said floodwater but crockery shards no assumed thaw no spindles small gears said fetlock the little house of ankle said gambrel said the circled ruminants mothered the water to the river & poured said those of us most in need tallowed our arms to reach under the loam & what be hopeful to hope something within reach reachable architecture undergirding something to pull up & be child

‡

no again listen again we had with us sons & daughters we cried over until wheat until scree we don't know it all was easier we us i wanted to remnant to narrative an order as if a woven thing to read catasterism for each it will tell it to to tell it but no response the fields left fallow the fields charred lintel

‡

not omenfowl not auspice boned but
hear the wind through them

‡

little said how they began apart less how
they knew to drop to scree or loess still
young enough to know their form from
milk know enough to gum dirt & tell
bones until ossein until jawbone yoked
their teeth nacre it's told bones naturally
rut it's instinctual body instinctually lithic
takes to mountain set the table set the
bones

Aloe
Andrew Porter

~

That August after our son was born I bought six or seven large aloe plants and placed them in these very beautiful and very expensive black planters. I couldn't actually afford these planters at the time—I could barely afford the aloe plants—but as soon as I saw them at the nursery down the street from our house I felt that I had to have them. I have always liked succulents, but especially aloes with their dark green leaves, sprouting out like octopus arms, pointy and jagged along the edges but soft and fleshy when you squeeze them, filled with that mysterious green gel with its curative powers and distinctive sour smell. It was nice to have them nearby. I liked looking at them out the window in the mornings as I drank my coffee, sitting there in those modern black planters with their clean edges and dark soil. I barely had to water them that summer—maybe once a month at most—but in the winter, as the weather began to change, I noticed them drooping a bit and browning along the edges. The man I'd bought them from at the nursery had told me I might have to bring them inside once the temperature dropped; even in a warm and arid climate like San Antonio, the winters could be too much for them. So I began bringing them inside on colder days and arranging them around our living room. Our house was small and my wife wasn't happy about this. She claimed that our living space was beginning to take on a "wet, fertile smell." Still, having just brought a child into the world, it somehow felt wrong to suddenly abandon these plants, to leave them outside in the cold where they would surely die. I suggested that we could think of these plants as new members of our family. We could even name them. But my wife had stopped listening by then.

"I don't want to live in a green house," she said. "Okay?" And that seemed to be the end of the conversation.

And so, later that day, I took all but one of the aloes back to the nursery where they were warmly received and given a new home back in their old corner. I didn't get my money back, of course, but by then I was simply happy that they had a home again, that they had a place where they could grow and prosper.

Driving home that evening, I thought about my son who I'd left sleeping in his crib in the living room next to my wife, who was also asleep on the couch, and across from the one solitary aloe plant in the corner—the one I'd kept, the smallest and the most beautiful. *Aloe nobilis*. His unnamed brother.

__HUATL
Art Por Díaz

~

if unknown:
- spanish is a modern language with a foundation in latin
- word sodium comes from latin
- Na is the chemical element for sodium
- Nahuatl (or uto-nahuatl) is the family name for the indigenous languages of the Americas

        Na_____
        Na_____
        Na_____

i came by plane
at the airport
i was purchased a teddy bear
tongue bare
ojos on osos
this one this two
this three this forced

tongue
licked the syllables
sweet honey
"Yes"
the bee sstung
but the bear was in my arms

grade school
immigration came
slowly
this one this two

this three we forced
ourselves to the bathroom stalls
standing tall on toilets
time trickled like sweat
this one this two
this three this long

feet shuffle silently one toilet over
"ssh"
the bee sstung
tense tiny bodies
this one this two
this three this foot slips

"swallowed pain"
the bee sstung
falling hurts
bruise on knee, pens whose ink broke within
quietly this one this two
this three these kids
held their fears
like teddy bears
hoping they wouldn't betray us
those grizzly bears

                Na____
                Na____
                Na____

go away!
                            ¡Xiauh!
      leave me alone!
                            ¡Xiauh!

CONTRIBUTORS
~

SEAN CHO A. is the author of *American Home* (Autumn House, 2021), winner of the Autumn House Press chapbook contest. His work can be future found or ignored in *Copper Nickel*, *Prairie Schooner*, *The Massachusetts Review*, and *Nashville Review*, among others. Sean is a graduate of the MFA program at the University of California at Irvine and a Ph.D. student at the University of Cincinnati. Find him at @phlat_soda.

ASHLEIGH A. ALLEN is a poet, writer, researcher, and educator. She is currently a Ph.D. student in Curriculum and Pedagogy at OISE, University of Toronto.

VALERIA AMIRKHANYAN was born in 1991 in a closed Siberian town where nuclear waste was stored. She believes that deepening the connection between nature and the real world makes people careful with nature. The land is for plants, not for nuclear burial grounds. Valeria has been managing the "Art Garden" studio for one year, where she teaches painting and grows more than fifty plant species.

Reporter, photographer, and visual artist, GUILHERME BERGAMINI is Brazilian and graduated with a degree in journalism. His works dialogue between memory and social-political criticism. He believes in photography as the potential transforming agent of society. Awarded in national and international competitions, Guilherme Bergamini has participated in collective exhibitions in fifty countries.

JOHN BLAIR has published six books, most recently *Playful Song Called Beautiful* (University of Iowa Press, 2016) as well as poems & stories in *Colorado Review*, *Poetry*, *The Sewanee Review*, *The Antioch Review*, *New Letters*, and elsewhere. His seventh book, *The Aphelion Elegies*, is forthcoming next spring from Main Street Rag Press.

CIARAN COOPER's writing has appeared in *Salamander*, *The Pinch*, *Midwest Review*, and *Fiction Southeast*, among other journals. Cooper holds an

MFA from Bennington College. He has won several awards for his writing, including the University of Madison Writers' Institute annual fiction and poetry contests and *The Pinch*'s annual fiction contest. He's also received two artist fellowship awards from the Illinois Arts Council and an Artist-in-Residence Fellowship from Salem Art Works. "Eddie's Mom" is from his upcoming collection, *One Time*. He has also recently completed a novel.

ANGIE CRUZ is the 2021 Gina Berriault Award recipient and the author of the novels *Dominicana* and *How Not To Drown In A Glass Of Water*. She's the editor-in-chief of the literary journal *Aster(ix)* and teaches creative writing at the University of Pittsburgh. These micro-stories were written while in-residence at the Siena Art Institute in Italy during summer 2015.

A. A. DEFREESE's work appears in *Many Mountains Moving*, *Puerto del Sol*, and *Southwestern American Literature*. Her poetry manuscript is forthcoming in 2023.

After receiving his MFA in creative writing from Emerson College, JACQUES DENAULT began teaching first year writing as an adjunct lecturer at Merrimack College, where he is currently employed. His work has previously appeared in *Hobart*, *Meniscus*, and *Writer's Digest*.

ART POR DÍAZ (loosely translates to "Art for days"), is known for their award-winning 10-minute play "A La Roro." Díaz is a graduate of Chabot College, Gonzaga University, and is currently pursuing an MA and MFA at San Francisco State University. Díaz once fought a squirrel and sea lion (not simultaneously) and tells people they won but in truth, at best, the squirrel and sea lion would say Díaz kept it competitive. You can find Díaz on socials using the handle @artpordiaz on everything.

MEGAN ERICKSON is the author of the non-fiction book *Class War*, and is currently at work on her first book of poems. She is an editor at *Jacobin* magazine and has worked in a preschool and taught elementary and middle school for many years. Her work has appeared in *The Guardian*, *The Nation*, *BOMB*, *Indiana Review* and *Beloit Poetry Journal*. She lives in Florida with her husband and two sons.

KATE GARDINER is an illustrator living on Peaks Island, ME. Kate is currently working on illustrating her first picture book, which is forthcoming from HarperCollins/Balzer + Bray. Publication is scheduled for fall 2023. She is represented by Steven Malk of Writers House Literary Agency and is an advisory board member to the Illustration Institute.

MARY HENN is a Midwest-based journalist and poet. She is the recipient of an AWP Intro Journals Award and recently earned an MFA from the University of Missouri, Kansas City. She is the current associate editor at *Kansas City* magazine.

SAÚL HERNÁNDEZ is a queer writer from San Antonio, TX who was raised by undocumented parents. Saúl has an MFA in creative writing from the University of Texas at El Paso. He's the winner of the 2021 Two Sylvias Press Chapbook Prize chosen by Victoria Chang. His poems have been nominated for a Pushcart Prize and Best of The Net. Saúl's work is forthcoming/featured in *Frontier Poetry*, *Poet Lore*, *Foglifter*, *Oyster River Pages*, *Cherry Tree*, and elsewhere.

NATASHA HUEY is a poet, teaching artist, and project manager. Natasha has performed on stages across the nation and beyond including the Oracle Arena in Oakland, the Warfield Theater in San Francisco, the Saban Theatre in Los Angeles, and Atlantis, the Palm in Dubai. She has performed on five nationally-competing spoken word poetry teams and was awarded "Best Poet" at collegiate nationals in 2013. At Youth Speaks, she organized Brave New Voices, the largest international youth poetry festival in the world, and managed campaigns that applied youth voice to changing public conversations about systemic injustices including environmental drivers of health disparities, educational inequity, and more. Natasha is currently an Artist Mentor at Performing Arts Workshop, co-founder of The Root Slam, and co-founder of the Write Home Project.

LIZ IVERSEN was born in the Philippines and grew up in South Dakota. Her writing has appeared in *Creative Nonfiction*, *Room*, *J Journal: New Writing on Justice*, and elsewhere. She has an MA in English with a creative writing emphasis from San Francisco State University and has received support from *Tin House* and the Maine Writers & Publishers Alliance. You can find her online at liziversen.com.

Until recently, NICHOLAS KARAVATOS was an assistant professor of poetics at the Arab American University of Palestine near Jenin in The West Bank. He was a U.S. Ambassador's Distinguished Scholar to Ethiopia in 2018 at Bahir Dar University, and from 2006 through 2017, an assistant professor of creative writing at The American University of Sharjah in the United Arab Emirates. At the Modern College of Business and Science in Muscat, Sultanate of Oman, he was a senior lecturer in humanities from 2001 through 2006. His first year as an expat worker was on the faculty of the Fujairah Technical School in the UAE from 2000 to 2001. Karavatos is a graduate of Humboldt State University in Arcata and New College of California in San Francisco.

STEFAN KARLSSON received his MFA in Poetry from the University of California, Irvine. His work has appeared in *Sugar House Review*, *Tar River Poetry*, and *Spillway*. He lives in Portland, OR.

PATRICK KINDIG currently teaches in the University Writing Program at Brandeis University. He is the author of the poetry chapbook *all the catholic gods* (Seven Kitchens Press, 2019) and the micro-chapbook *Dry Spell* (Porkbelly Press, 2016), and his creative work has recently appeared in *Colorado Review*, *The Chattahoochee Review*, *Shenandoah*, *Washington Square Review*, and other journals.

RON KOERTGE is the current poet laureate of South Pasadena, CA.

NATHAN KOSTA is a visual artist, educator, and photographic technology researcher based in the San Francisco Bay Area. His work explores issues relating to surveillance capitalism, photographic image recognition, machine learning, and land use.

CATHERINE KYLE is the author of *Shelter in Place* (Spuyten Duyvil, 2019), which received an honorable mention for the Idaho Book of the Year Award, and other poetry collections. Her writing has appeared or is forthcoming in *Bellingham Review*, *Colorado Review*, *Mid-American Review*, and other journals, and has been honored by the Idaho Commission on the Arts, the Alexa Rose Foundation, and other organizations. She was the winner of the 2019-2020 COG Poetry Award and a finalist for the 2021 *Mississippi Review* Prize in poetry. She is an assistant professor of English at DigiPen Institute of Technology.

When he's not writing, SEAN MASCHMANN teaches history at Langara College in Vancouver, BC. This is his first published story. You can find him at www.seanmaschmann.com.

CAMERON MORENO, a writer of fiction and poetry, holds an MFA from Western Kentucky University. A Pushcart Prize nominee, his work is featured in *Passages North*, *The Hunger*, and elsewhere, and is anthologized in Cutthroat's *Puro Chicanx Writers of the 21st Century*. He was born and raised in Corpus Christi, Texas.

HEMA PADHU's short fiction has appeared in *Fourteen Hills*, *American Literary Review*, *Tahoma Literary Review*, *Litro Magazine*, and more. A 2019 Fellow of the San Francisco Writers Grotto, she lives and works in San Francisco.

ANDREW PORTER is the author of the short story collections *The Theory of Light and Matter* (Vintage/Penguin Random House) and *The Disappeared* (forthcoming from Knopf in 2022), and the novel *In Between Days* (Knopf). His short stories have appeared in *The Pushcart Prize* anthology, *Ploughshares*, *One Story*, *The Southern Review*, *The Threepenny Review*, and on NPR's *Selected Shorts*. Currently, he teaches fiction writing and directs the Creative Writing Program at Trinity University in San Antonio.

MARY LYNN REED's fiction has appeared in *Mississippi Review*, *Colorado Review*, *Free State Review*, and many other places. She has an MFA in creative writing from the University of Maryland. She lives in western New York with her wife, and together they co-edit the online literary journal *MoonPark Review*.

LAURA RITLAND is an Asian Canadian/American poet, teacher, and scholar living on Huichin, Ohlone land (Berkeley). Her debut collection *East and West* (Véhicule Press, 2018) was shortlisted for the Pat Lowther Memorial Award and she has served twice as a teaching fellow with the Bay Area's New Literary Project.

ALEX WELLS SHAPIRO (he/him) is a poet and artist from the Hudson Valley, living in Chicago. He reads submissions for *Frontier Poetry*, serves as Business and Grants Manager for *Another Chicago Magazine*, and co-curates Exhibit B: A Reading Series presented by The Guild Literary Complex. His debut poetry collection, *Insect Architecture*, is forthcoming in Spring 2022 with Unbound Edition Press. More of his work may be found at www.alexwellsshapiro.com.

Making art has been an almost impossible pursuit and yet CHRISTOPHER STROPLE remains determined to such a pursuit. Neither an identity nor a "calling," instead it endures as an exercise that, for him, simultaneously makes meaning and also records experience. His art is partially derived from a fondness for color and an affection for aesthetics. Numerous cultural influences inform him and a commitment to social justice provides continuous inspiration for his creative work.

EDWARD MICHAEL SUPRANOWICZ is the grandson of Irish and Russian/Ukrainian immigrants. He grew up on a small farm in Appalachia. He has a graduate background in painting and printmaking. Some of his artwork has recently or will soon appear in *Fish Food*, *Streetlight*, *Another Chicago*

Magazine, The Door Is a Jar, The Phoenix, and other journals. Edward is also a published poet.

B.P. SUTTON is the author of the chapbooks *Monument* (Press 254, 2020), *[something billeted, something treatise]* (Oxblood Press, 2018) and *Then, the Unabridged* (Black Warrior Review Chapbook Series, 2013). His poetry won the Kay Murphy Prize from the University of New Orleans and *Bayou Magazine,* judged by Dawn Lundy Martin. Other poems have recently appeared or are forthcoming in *Best New Poets, Fence, The Literary Review,* and *Volt,* among others.

In 2009, **DON SWARTZENTRUBER** started illustrating Christian apologetics with sequential art. His home was the hub for theological discussion groups and at Grace College and Seminary he taught art majors to storyboard their faith testimony. For over five years he wrote and drew short stories titled, "Sermons." Eventually, through his study, Swartzentruber became skeptical of Biblical fundamentalism. In 2015 his studio plan changed to a graphic novel of his own religious deconstruction.

GRACE WAGNER, winner of an Academy of American Poets Prize in 2020, is a recent graduate of the University of Houston MFA program in poetry where they received a certificate in women, gender, and sexuality studies, with a focus on feminist ecopoetics, queer studies, and disability feminisms. Their art has been featured in *The Adroit Journal,* and their poetry in *Atlanta Review, Salmagundi Magazine, The Missouri Review, The Offing, Hayden's Ferry Review,* and elsewhere. For more, visit www.gracewagnerpoet.com.

ERIN WILSON's poems have recently appeared or are forthcoming in *Reed Magazine, The South Carolina Review, CV2, The Emerson Review,* and in numerous other publications and anthologies internationally. Her first collection is *At Home with Disquiet;* her second, *Blue,* is forthcoming. She lives in a small town on Robinson-Huron Treaty territory in Northern Ontario, the traditional lands of the Anishnawbek.

AMBER WONG is an environmental engineer in Seattle who writes about culture, identity, and her firsthand knowledge about hazardous waste sites. Recent work appeared in *Pangyrus, Creative Nonfiction, Stanford Magazine,* and *Tahoma Literary Review,* among others. Amber earned an MFA from Lesley University and is working on a memoir. (https://amberwong.com)

CANDICE WUEHLE is the author of the novel *MONARCH* (Soft Skull, 2022) as well as the poetry collections *Fidelitoria: Fixed or Fluxed* (11:11,

2021); 2020 Believer Magazine Book Award finalist and SPD bestseller, *Death Industrial Complex* (Action Books, 2020); and *BOUND* (Inside the Castle Press, 2018). Her writing has appeared in *Best American Experimental Writing 2020*, *The Iowa Review*, *Joyland*, *Black Warrior Review*, *Tarpaulin Sky*, *The Volta*, *The Bennington Review*, and *The New Delta Review*. She holds an MFA in poetry from the Iowa Writers' Workshop and Ph.D. in creative writing from the University of Kansas. Candice currently teaches in the Jackson Center for Creative Writing at Hollins University.

SF STATE

Department of Creative Writing

Established in 1955, we offer full-time and part-time M.A. and M.F.A. tracks in creative nonfiction, fiction, literary translation, playwriting, and poetry.

Write with Us

Welcoming our new George and Judy Marcus Endowed Chairs

Joseph Cassara
Tonya M. Foster

Core Faculty:

Michelle Carter
Nona Caspers
May-lee Chai
Maxine Chernoff
Carolina De Robertis

Paul Hoover
Andrew Joron
Michael David Lukas
Chanan Tigay

APPLY TO AN MA/MFA IN CREATIVE WRITING

JOSEPH CASSARA — THE HOUSE OF IMPOSSIBLE BEAUTIES

PAUL HOOVER — THE BOOK OF UNNAMED THINGS

TONYA M. FOSTER — A SWARM OF BEES IN HIGH COURT

MAXINE CHERNOFF | CAMERA

NONA CASPERS — THE FIFTH WOMAN

MICHELLE CARTER — HILLARY AND SOON-YI SHOP FOR TIES

MAY-LEE CHAI — USEFUL PHRASES FOR IMMIGRANTS

CAROLINA DE ROBERTIS — CANTORAS

CHANAN TIGAY — THE LOST BOOK OF MOSES

ANDREW JORON — TRANCE ARCHIVE

MICHAEL DAVID LUKAS — THE LAST WATCHMAN OF OLD CAIRO

Recent Visiting Writers:

NoViolet Bulawayo
Juli Delgado Lopera
Tongo Eisen-Martin
Cristina García

R.O. Kwon
Layli Long Soldier
Tommy Orange
Ingrid Rojas Contreras

AT SF STATE WWW.SFSU.EDU

think *yours* is good? submit!

February 15th – June 15th
www.fourteenhills.submittable.com*

visual art •
fiction • poetry • creative nonfiction

more info., guidelines, interviews, essays:
www.14hills.net

for issues & purchases, please visit:
www.spdbooks.org

art:
"Pothos"
by
Wynn Nguyen

Fourteen Hills
THE SAN FRANCISCO STATE UNIVERSITY REVIEW

*For those without computer access, please mail your completed, neatly-printed manuscript with your name and contact information *year-round* to:

Fourteen Hills Press
SFSU Creative Writing Dept.
1600 Holloway Ave
San Francisco CA 94132

"Blends the traditional academic litmag with experimental writing in a slick, well-produced journal."
—Todd Dayton, MetroACTIVE

"That *Fourteen Hills* is able to consistently put together books full of quality and grace always astonishes me."
—Stephen Elliott

"Beautifully designed, impeccably edited, *Fourteen Hills* is one of those handful of literary journals doing the important work of keeping American writing alive and new."
—George Saunders

"*Fourteen Hills* might just as aptly be titled 'Fourteen Styles,' such a broad spectrum of approaches to narrative and poetics does it present."
—Mark Cunningham, NewPages.com

IR

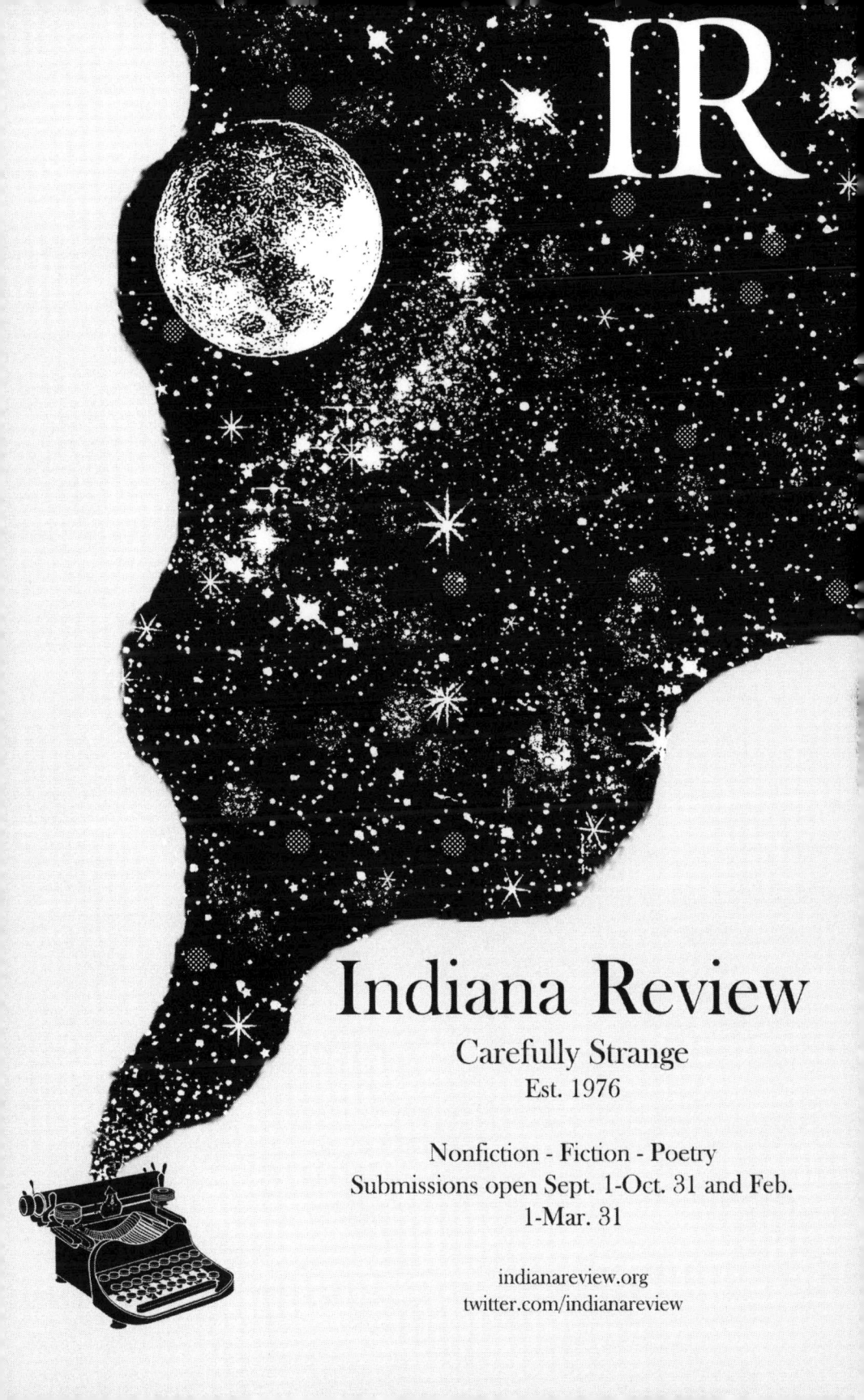

Indiana Review

Carefully Strange
Est. 1976

Nonfiction - Fiction - Poetry
Submissions open Sept. 1-Oct. 31 and Feb. 1-Mar. 31

indianareview.org
twitter.com/indianareview